The Arrogant Earl of Denfield

HISTORICAL REGENCY ROMANCE NOVEL

Sally Forbes

Table of Contents

Prologue..4

Chapter One..11

Chapter Two 17

Chapter Three..24

Chapter Four...29

Chapter Five..37

Chapter Six..45

Chapter Seven...50

Chapter Eight 56

Chapter Nine...62

Chapter Ten 69

Chapter Eleven..77

Chapter Twelve...84

Chapter Thirteen...90

Chapter Fourteen 98

Chapter Fifteen..103

Chapter Sixteen 109

Chapter Seventeen 114

Chapter Nineteen 125

Chapter Twenty 130

Chapter Twenty-One 135

Chapter Twenty-Two 141

Chapter Twenty-Three..148

Chapter Twenty-Four..154

Epilogue 159

Prologue

Anne looked out of the window as her sister's carriage rolled away from their father's manor house and felt the tears begin to burn behind her eyes. As delighted as she was for Netty's marriage, she felt herself even more a spinster than she already was. Her father had given up on her completely and now with Netty wed and she the only one remaining in the house with him, her chances of finding happiness were almost entirely gone. There was the very slim hope that she might meet a gentleman in the vicinity of her father's estate but given that she was acquainted with all the neighbours already, the chances of that were very poor indeed.

Pulling out her handkerchief, Anne dabbed at her eyes, relieved that she was alone so that no-one would see her tears.

"I can hardly believe that Netty is wed!"

Anne crumpled up her handkerchief in her hand as she turned to greet her aunt who had come through the door of the drawing room, a broad smile on her face. "Yes, Aunt. It is quite wonderful, is it not?"

"And when are you to marry?" her aunt asked, tilting her head as Anne quickly looked away, aware of how quickly her face heated. "Your father is to take you back to London next Season, is he?"

Shaking her head, Anne looked out of the window again in the hope that her aunt would not see the tears in her eyes. "I think father has quite given up on me, Aunt. After all, I am one and twenty and therefore nothing more than a spinster."

"Oh, nonsense!" Lady Mayhew waved her hand wildly, an action which Anne caught out of the corner of her eye. "I was *two* and twenty before I met Viscount Mayhew and three and twenty before we wed! You are not a spinster yet."

"Yes, she is."

Anne closed her eyes tightly as the voice of her father rolled through the room, the heavy weight of his chagrin seating itself on her shoulders.

"You know as well as I, Lady Mayhew, that Anne is much too old now to be considered by any gentleman."

"That is ridiculous," came the firm reply, as Anne opened her eyes, one hand pressed against her stomach to steady herself though she did not dare bring her gaze around to where her father stood. "As I was just saying to Anne, I myself was not wed until I was three and twenty!"

Lord Ellon let out a snort of what sounded like ridicule and Anne's stomach tightened all over again. "Which was much too old, Lady Mayhew. Quite why Lord Mayhew took to you at that age, I shall never understand."

It was just like her father to be rude and inconsiderate though Anne's face burned with embarrassment all the same.

"Because he fell in love with me," Lady Mayhew replied, a laughing softness in her voice which brushed up against Lord Ellon's dark tones. "And we have been very happy and contented together for many years. Therefore, I will not agree with you that Anne here is unable to find herself a good match at her age. She must be given opportunity, that is all!"

"She has been given opportunity!" came the loud exclamation, which was then followed by a guffaw. "Good gracious, do you not know that Anne has had three Seasons without a single gentleman seeking to court her?"

Anne wanted to sink down into a pile of skirts on the floor, such was her shame. She had watched as her two younger sisters had both found suitable matches of their own – with Netty being the latter – while she herself stood back and wondered how she could exude the same elegance and ease of manner which they displayed. Her father had always criticized her, had always told her that she was lacking in one way or another – particularly in relation to her younger sisters – and thus, she had found herself tongue-tied in any conversation with a gentleman, sure that she was going to say the wrong thing or speak out of turn given the heavy criticism of her father. She shrank back, certain that her appearance was not as perfect as it ought to be, that the gown she wore or the color of it did nothing to enhance her appearance – again, all because of the criticism of her father. Her two younger sisters had not suffered in the same way for Lord Ellon, for whatever reason, seemed to think her the very worst out of the

5

three and had pushed all of his frustrations upon her rather than upon them.

If only mother was here. Anne's eyes burned with fresh tears as her aunt and her father continued to discuss her situation. How much she missed her dear, sweet mother who, some years ago, had taken herself to visit her sister up in Scotland and, thereafter, had never returned. Anne herself was forbidden to speak of the situation to anyone for her father had made it quite clear that she was to remain silent, though that did not prevent her from writing many letters to her mother whenever she could. They were always responded to with her mother always apologizing for her prolonged absence but never giving reason for it. She assured Anne, Charlotte and Netty of her love and begged them not to think poorly of her but that was all that had ever been said by way of explanation.

"*I* shall take Anne to London for the Season."

Anne turned quickly, all thought of her mother going from her mind as she stared at her aunt, seeing how she had her hands at her hips and her head lifted in a triumphant gesture.

"Why should you waste your time on Anne?" Lord Ellon retorted as though Anne herself was not standing between them. "Nothing will come of it, I promise you! Besides which, it is good for me to have her around the house. Since her mother has not yet returned from her prolonged visit to Lady Arnette, I require Anne to keep this house running as it ought."

Closing her eyes again briefly, Anne's shoulders dropped, her heart growing heavy all over again. There was not to be any Season for her, not again. Her father was quite right, she had failed to find a suitable match these last few Seasons, so why should she be given any further responsibility?

Though, would it not be different alongside your aunt? said a quiet voice in her head. *Would it not be quite wonderful?*

"Do stop complaining about this, Ellon." Lady Mayhew sniffed, turning her head to Anne. "Anne herself wishes to join me and you will be able to deal very well with living alone, I am sure. After all, it is not a situation which is likely to change at any moment, is it?"

Anne felt rather than saw the anger which quickly flooded the room, feeling the atmosphere grow thicker, the darkness

6

surrounding them all. Lady Mayhew and Anne's own mother were sisters and clearly, her mother had written to Lady Mayhew to explain what was happening with her own circumstances at present – and Lord Ellon was all too aware of it.

"You shall *not* take my daughter to – "

"Yes, I shall." Lady Mayhew lifted her eyebrow, her head cocked to one side, hands still tight at her waist. "And you *shall* agree, Lord Ellon. What is more, you shall give me enough funds to make certain that Anne has new gowns, gloves and shawls, as well as pin money."

Anne looked to her father, catching her bottom lip between her teeth. Her father was a tall and imposing figure, his shoulders broad and a deep shadow spreading out from him as though it wanted to engulf them all. There was a tension and a tightness in his jaw that had not been there before. Anne's heart thudded wildly, seeing her aunt and her father go up against each other while she herself felt nothing but anxious. Looking down at her hands, she gripped them both together and squeezed, unable to lift her head to look back at her father.

"And if I do not?" The challenge in Lord Ellon's voice had Anne's gaze jumping to her aunt, seeing her frown.

"If you do not give me Anne to take with me to London for the Season, then I am afraid that there are some circumstances which I think will entertain the *ton* a great deal."

"Circumstances?"

"Yes," Lady Mayhew replied, her eyebrow arched. "I might have to tell the *ton* that Lady Ellon has taken a *prolonged* leave of absence from her husband's estate. And I might also have to tell them my considerations as to why that might be."

Lord Ellon's face went scarlet, his eyes blazing with anger as he stood as tall as he could and Anne felt herself shrinking inwardly, though Lady Mayhew seemed entirely calm given the way she simply looked back at Lord Ellon without a single flicker of concern in her gaze.

"How dare you think to even threaten such thing?" Lord Ellon spat, coming a little closer to Lady Mayhew. "Besides which, you are a fool to even *suggest* that you will do that for in doing so, you will injure your niece! Anne will have a stain upon her reputation and – "

"Which will matter very little given that you have decided that she ought to be a spinster," replied Lady Mayhew, calmly. "And your other two daughters are wed and settled so it will not injure them."

Anne looked again to her father, her worry growing so severely, she felt her breath tighten in her chest. She knew all too well the temper that her father possessed and the last thing she desired was for it to be thrown upon her aunt, given that Lady Mayhew was only trying to do her some good. She had no expectation that her father would relent for he was always determined, always unwilling to brook even a single argument, a single word against his desires. With a small sigh, Anne turned her attention back to the window and waited for her aunt's defeat.

"I will have no part of this."

Her eyes flared as Lord Ellon continued to speak, a fierce, burning, furious hope building in her heart, offering her something she had never even imagined might be for her.

"This will be her last Season. If you do this, if you take her and have no success, then you will never complain to me about this again. You will never ask for any further time with her. Do I make myself clear?"

"Quite. Though I expect that money from you also, Ellon. I have seen how you have treated your eldest daughter and how differently you have treated the other two. You ought to be ashamed of yourself in that."

"I do not know – "

"Do not pretend that you have no understanding of what I am talking about," Lady Mayhew interrupted Lord Ellon sharply, leaving Anne to catch her breath in astonishment. "You have berated her, criticized her and shamed her simply because she looks the most like her own, dear mama. Is that not your reason for your harsh treatment?" Her voice rose, echoing around the room as tears began to pour into Anne's eyes all over again. "But I will give her the opportunities that you have stolen from her by your hard-heartedness towards her, I will give Anne the confidence she has so often lacked. And I *will* have her married, settled and happy by the end of the Season. I can promise you that."

Anne's heart swelled with such a love for her aunt, with such an overwhelming happiness that she wanted to throw herself into

8

Lady Mayhew's embrace but, instead, she wrapped her arms about her waist and waited for the conversation to come to an end.

"I highly doubt that!" The sneer in Lord Ellon's voice took away some of Anne's joy though she fought hard to keep it. "I have very little hope of your success."

"Then I place a bet upon your disbelief."

Anne turned quickly, her eyes wide, wanting to warn her aunt away from doing such a thing, wanting to tell her not to push Lord Ellon any more, but Lady Mayhew merely glanced at her and then smiled with a confidence that Anne could not understand.

"If I am successful, then you will offer Anne three times the dowry you have for her at present."

Anne sucked in a breath, shock rifling through her.

"And if I fail, then I shall repay you all the funds that have been spent on Anne for the Season," Lady Mayhew finished. "What say you to that, Ellon?"

Forcing herself to look into her father's face, Anne saw the cruel curl of his lip, the laughing mockery in his eyes and felt herself begin to panic. She had already tried and failed at the Season before. What was it that her aunt thought she could to in order to force success upon her? She tried to speak, tried to tell Lady Mayhew not to do such a thing but before she could do so, Lord Ellon waved one hand and made his declaration.

"*Two* times her dowry at present, not three."

"No," Lady Mayhew returned, quickly. "Three and not a penny less. I have no doubt that you have offered her a very poor dowry already so such a thing will not strain you."

Lord Ellon considered and then shrugged, his shoulders lifting and falling back again. "Very well. As I have said, it will not be of any difficulty to me for I am certain you shall fail."

Lady Mayhew chuckled and Anne was surprised to see the flash of a frown crossing her father's expression. Could it be that he had a little doubt in his heart? That he was uncertain about what he had just done?

"Very good, Ellon. I shall have the papers drawn up and we shall sign them together – oh yes, you need not look so surprised! You are not a gentleman known to keep his word and therefore, I shall have it all formalized and the like, so you cannot escape it when I bring Anne and her betrothed to you." She smiled and then

9

looked to Anne. "Come now, Anne, there is much for us to discuss. The Season shall soon be upon us and I want to be as prepared as we can be."

Anne moved towards her aunt on legs that trembled, trying her best not to look into the foreboding face of her father. Lady Mayhew continued to speak as she led Anne out into the hallway, away from Lord Ellon, away from the dark atmosphere and, as they walked, Anne slowly felt the tension within her begin to fade.

"Am I really to go to London with you, Aunt?"

She stopped walking, turning her head to look up at Lady Mayhew who quickly slipped an arm around her shoulders, comforting her.

"Yes, of course you are, my dear. And more than that, you shall find yourself courted, engaged, wed and happy." Her eyes softened. "I promise you that."

Chapter One

Anne shook her head. "I don't think I can do this, Aunt."

"Of course you can."

Looking down at herself, Anne shook her head again, this time all the more fervently. "I cannot! This is not the right colour for me and the cut of the gown is – "

"It is the very height of fashion," Lady Mayhew interrupted, smoothly. "Yes, it is a little different to what you are used to but I assure you, it is just as it ought to be. And as for the colour, given your raven hair and bright eyes, this gown will suit your green eyes perfectly."

Anne blinked furiously, aware that there was something like panic lodged in her chest. Her gown was a gentle turquoise and had lace trim at the sleeves and the neck. To her, it felt as though she was revealing a little too much of her *decolletage* and the color was much too vivid for someone such as her. And yet, her aunt was insistent.

"I do not want to argue, Aunt," she said, as the modiste smiled and nodded in evident great appreciation of the gown upon Anne's frame, "but I am not sure that this will be the right gown for someone such as I to wear."

Lady Mayhew's expression softened and she reached out to squeeze Anne's hand. "My dear girl, you are still very much afraid, are you not?"

Anne wanted to shake her head no, wanted to say that she was more than a little contented but try as she might, she could not bring herself to lie to her aunt. "I confess that I am continually afraid of what my father would think."

"Though he is not here," Lady Mayhew reminded her. "And he shall not set foot in London this Season, as well you know."

"He might," Anne protested, weakly. "He might decide to attend London so that he can watch me fail, just as I have done these previous years."

Lady Mayhew shrugged. "Then if he does, he shall come to

see your success, do you not think?"

Anne blinked, still struggling to find the same confidence within herself as was within her aunt. "I do not know. I am almost afraid to hope!"

"Another consequence of spending so much time with your father, I think." Lady Mayhew sighed heavily. "My dear girl, I am sorry that so much has been set upon your shoulders. It is the very reason your mother has removed herself to Scotland, though I know that it broke her heart to leave the three of you with your father."

Anne swallowed hard, questions beginning to arise in her mind. She had not spoken of her mother to anyone, not for a long time, for fear of what her father would do should he discover it. But she could trust her aunt, could she not? "Did she always think to leave us?"

"Oh, no!" Lady Mayhew's eyes flared wide. "My dear, she did not expect for a moment to have left you all for so long. Do recall that I have visited her and spoken with her at length on this matter."

Nodding slowly, Anne considered for a few moments. "You mentioned to me in one of your letters that you visited Scotland."

"I did. I spent the first three months of the year with both of my sisters." Lady Mayhew smiled rather sadly, her gaze going away from Anne. "I do think that your mother is a good deal more herself than she has been in some years. I spoke to her about her absence, about the length of time she has been away and the torment it brought her gave me such pain, I regretted ever speaking to her of it!"

"But why could she not return?"

Lady Mayhew closed her eyes briefly. "Your father is the cause of her pain, Anne." Opening her eyes, she looked back at her. "I will speak plainly, for you will understand it and I believe it will help you in your present struggle: your father threatened your mother's very life and it is for that reason that she ran to Scotland."

A tremor shook Anne's frame, her breathing becoming quick and shallow as she looked back into her aunt's solemn face, seeing the truth hidden in her expression.

"I would not have told you for any other reason than

understanding," Lady Mayhew continued, quietly. "If she returned home, she was uncertain as to whether she would remain alive for any length of time. You father's fury, his anger, has always been hot and uncertain and, sadly, directed towards her. You cannot imagine her torment, given how much she loved her daughters but how much she feared for her own life."

Anne swallowed hard, tears pricking her eyes. "Thank you for telling me." Her voice was weak and thin. "I do appreciate the truth, Aunt. I have always missed my mother and could never truly understand why she left for Scotland... though I did wonder if it might be something to do with father."

Lady Mayhew blinked rapidly, clearing away tears. "She loves you desperately, as do I. In truth, I should have come to your aid long before now. I merely thought that since your sisters had found success, you would too but in your own time. I did not realise that your father thought you devoid of purpose just because you had reached a certain age."

Anne laughed rather ruefully. "I have always been encouraged towards failure."

"But not any longer." Lady Mayhew tilted her head, regarding her. "You truly do look like your mother."

A knot formed in Anne's throat and she looked away, spreading her hands out either side as she took in the gown once more. "If you believe that this will suit me, Aunt, then I will be glad to wear it." She heard the slight tremor in her voice, caught the faint whisper of worry in her words but lifted her chin and gave her reflection a nod of determination. "I *shall* wear whatever you think best."

"Wonderful!" Lady Mayhew beamed at her, the tears in her eyes now quickly forgotten. "Then let me next encourage you to try on *this* gown. Yes, it is not cream or white as your father would expect, but a soft blue. I think it will suit you very well."

Anne turned to look at the gown the modiste had brought out and though the color and the cut worried her – as the gown she currently wore had done – she found in herself a tiny wedge of confidence and thus, gave it a nod. "I shall try it on, certainly."

"Excellent." Lady Mayhew smiled at her again, her eyes alight with happiness. "You shall find yourself anew this Season, my dear Anne. It will truly be the happiest Season you have ever experienced!"

It was not until some hours had passed that Anne was finally able to step out of the modiste's shop alongside her aunt, finding herself suddenly rather tired though all she had done had been to stand and try on various gowns and other adornments. She was pleased, however, that she had managed to do all that her aunt had asked of her and though her confidence was still lacking, though she found herself questioning almost everything that her aunt had encouraged her to try on, Anne had fought against such worries and had won.

"Now, your first ball is this evening," her aunt reminded her as they walked along the street, back towards the waiting carriage which was a short distance away. "There is much that we need to discuss and practice before then."

Anne nodded. "I confess, Aunt, that whenever a gentleman tries to speak with me, I find myself so caught up with fright that I can barely speak a word back to him." Her face grew hot as her aunt looked at her sharply, her lips pressing tight together for a moment. "I am embarrassed to say so but that is my great struggle."

"It is something that can be overcome, however." Lady Mayhew again spoke with a confidence and a determination that Anne wished would spread through her also, hating that her stomach was twisting and turning in all such directions. "You will need practice, as I have said, and you will also need to have only brief moments of conversation rather than thinking you must speak at length to any given gentleman."

Anne looked at her in surprise. "You do not think that I must find a good many things to talk about with a gentleman?" she asked, a little astonished. "My father has always instructed me to have at least five questions in mind which I am to ask any gentleman who seeks to speak with me. Five questions which will show an interest and prove that I am able to make excellent conversation."

Lady Mayhew laughed merrily and shook her head. "Goodness, no! You need not put such a weight upon yourself!

14

When I met Lord Mayhew for the first time, introductions were made and, thereafter, he asked me to dance. Do you know what our conversation was like that evening?"

"No, I do not."

"It was nothing at all!" Lady Mayhew replied, her expression still one of mirth. "He did not speak to me during our dance and I did not speak to him. Once it was at an end, he returned me to my sister and that was that. The next ball, he asked me to dance again but it was only through a distant acquaintance that our conversations finally began to grow. You need not worry so much, my dear girl. In fact..." Turning, she took both of Anne's hands in her own, looking Anne square in the eye. "I should like you, from this moment, to forget everything your father has told you. I should like you to put it all aside, to never think of it again. Instead, I should ask you to pretend that this is your first Season – though it is your first Season with *me*, I suppose – and that you do not know a single thing about what to do or how to act. I shall instruct you in everything and you need not think on what your father would do or what he would think of your actions ever again."

Anne swallowed hard, nodding slowly as her aunt searched her expression, perhaps looking for worry in Anne's expression.

"You can do that?"

"I – I think I can." Taking in a deep breath, Anne set her shoulders and nodded. "I know I can."

"That's exactly what I wanted to hear. I – "

"What do you think you're doing?"

Anne turned her head just in time to see a gentleman lurching out of a carriage, his shouted exclamation what had interrupted her aunt. Her eyes widened as the gentleman staggered forward, his feet tripping over themselves as another gentleman laughed raucously from the carriage behind him. Had he been pushed out of the carriage for some reason?

"It is a little early for such nonsense." Lady Mayhew's eyes narrowed slightly, her tongue clicking in disapproval. "Goodness, these sorts of gentlemen are certainly *not* the sort I shall be introducing you to this evening!"

Anne found herself studying both gentlemen, first the one in the carriage and the other who was, by now, attempting to climb back inside though he could not seem to get one foot onto the step so addled were his wits. The fellow in the carriage was laughing uproariously, his head thrown back, his shock of dark hair falling carelessly over his forehead when he looked back at his friend. The other gentleman was fair-haired and was slim and wiry, though he had not realized until now that he had lost his hat in the street. Releasing his grip from the carriage, he turned around and made to reach for it, only to fall over his feet again and crumple to the street.

"We should go away," Lady Mayhew said quickly, threading her arm through Anne's and beginning to hurry her away from both gentlemen. "Such behaviour is a disgrace and had I known their names, I would have gone to them and offered them such a scolding, it would have rung through all of London!"

Anne hid a smile, knowing full well that Lady Mayhew would have done such a thing without hesitation – and that the two gentlemen might have come to their senses because of it! All the same, however, she turned her head and glanced back at them, a little relieved to see that the fair-haired gentleman was now climbing back into the carriage and was no longer crumpled on the ground.

"Disgraceful," Lady Mayhew said again, as Anne turned her head back again. "Now, let us begin to think of what this evening will bring rather than considering these poor excuses for gentlemen! There is much to be achieved and much to learn... and what better time to start than this very moment!"

Anne smiled at her aunt, glad to hear the enthusiasm back in her voice. "I am willing to learn whatever you wish to teach me, Aunt," she said, trying to ignore the worry which threatened to pinch at her mind. "Including which sort of gentlemen to avoid!"

Lady Mayhew let out a tinkling laugh as they reached their own carriage. "Gentlemen who behave like *that* ought to be entirely ignored," she stated, firmly. "But have no fear, there will be many an example of excellent gentlemen this evening. Of that, I am quite sure."

Chapter Two

Peter ran one hand over his eyes and slumped back against the carriage squabs. He had laughed so hard, his chest hurt. "Will you sit down, Henley?"

His brother grinned at him. "I *am* sitting down. You have drunk so much, it seems as though you cannot tell whether I am sitting or standing!"

"I am well aware that you are *standing*." Though Peter had laughed at his brother's foolishness, he was not about to let Henley believe that he was as inebriated as he. "Sit *down*, Henley, before the carriage leaves and you fall over. You have done enough falling already!"

His brother frowned and, looking all about him, seemed to realize – albeit slowly – that Peter had been speaking the truth. With a grin, he seemed to half-fall, half-sit in the seat opposite Peter and then closed his eyes.

"You are *not* to cast up your accounts in this carriage, do you hear me?" Peter warned, seeing the color begin to drain from his brother's face as the carriage lurched back down the cobbled street towards Peter's townhouse. "I came to rescue you from Lord Yardley, as your message stated, only to find you so utterly overcome, you could barely stand! It would be shameful to then disgrace yourself in such a way."

Viscount Henley only let out a low groan, a line forming between his eyebrows as his face scrunched up into a frown.

"You are feeling unwell already?" Peter scowled and then shook his head. "Brother or not, I will have you out on the street if you *dare* think of being sick in my carriage."

"I will not cast up my accounts," Lord Henley mumbled, though Peter did not believe him given the color of his face. "Goodness, whyever did I send for you and your monstrosity of a carriage again?"

Peter sighed and closed his eyes, his mirth already leaving him. His brother and he had always been close given that there was only a year between their births, but of late, Henley had taken to keeping in poor company and his behavior was becoming a little more erratic. What was worse, he often called on Peter to come and rescue him from whatever situation he found himself in and, every time thus far, Peter had left what he himself had been doing and had come to the aid of his brother, even though he found himself rather displeased at the interruption.

"You sent for me because, as your message stated, Lord Yardley was forcing you to imbibe far too much brandy and was speaking of such dark things, you found yourself to be scared out of your wits."

"Oh." Lord Henley frowned, though his eyes remained closed. "It is just as well I always take my manservant with me. He is very good at sending you messages."

"Yes, he is," Peter agreed, dryly, "though I do not think that he is particularly pleased with the notion."

His brother snorted. "I do not care what it is that he thinks. He is to do as I instruct him and that is all." Lifting his head, his eyes opening suddenly, he smiled blandly at Peter. "Shall we stop at Whites? I am in mind of making a bet!"

"Certainly, we shall not," Peter replied, firmly, all hint of mirth now gone from his mind as he saw the ridiculousness of his brother's behavior. "It is the very worst of times to make a bet when one is as inebriated as you."

"You could always join me to make certain that I do not make any bets that are *too* ridiculous."

Peter rolled his eyes. "As though I should be glad to waste more of my time doing such a thing as that. In case you are unaware, brother, I was engaged in a matter of business when your message came. I was forced to leave that to come to your aid."

"Which is just as you ought to have done, given your standing as my brother."

Shaking his head, Peter looked out of the window rather than at his brother. He had caught sight of more than one disapproving look as he had laughed at his brother's attempts to climb back up into the carriage, though he had cared very little for what anyone thought. After all, it was not *he* who had fallen to the street. That was entirely his brother's doing and if Lord Henley wished to ruin his own reputation, then Peter could do nothing to prevent it. Yes, he would come to his aid but what Lord Henley chose to do was his own decision.

Though mayhap I ought to have been more sober-minded, he

18

considered, his mouth pulling to one side. *Perhaps in laughing along with him, perhaps in joviality, I have failed to show any sort of restraint or sober thinking.*

Closing his eyes and letting out a huff of breath, Peter tried to sort out one thought from another. He was not his brother's keeper, of course, but his heart would not permit him to ignore his brother when his request for help came. That being said, Peter was beginning to fear that this situation was repeating itself – and would continue to do so until either he refused to come to Lord Henley's aid, or until Lord Henley himself realized the foolishness of what he was doing.

"At last, we have arrived!"

It took Peter a moment to realize that his brother was quite correct and that they were now outside Peter's own townhouse, rather than the townhouse which belonged to his brother. "I will instruct the driver to take you back home."

"No, I shall join you."

Peter put out one hand, pressing his brother gently back into his seat as Lord Henley made to rise. "No, Henley, you shall not," he said, with more firmness than his brother had expected given the way his eyes rounded. "I am to return to the matter of business I am considering and cannot have any distractions. Are you to attend the ball this evening?"

Lord Henley frowned but nodded. "I think so."

"Lord and Lady Colinsdale's ball," Peter reminded him, though no flash of recognition came into his brother's expression. "Might I suggest, then, that you go home, rest and recover before this evening's festivities?" He did not give his brother time to answer, did not give him opportunity to agree or to disagree but instead, opened the carriage door and stepped out before quickly instructing the driver to return his brother to his own townhouse. Watching it roll away, he sighed inwardly and turned to walk into his own house.

"Your brother, again?"

A gentle voice greeted him as he came into the hallway, quickly handing the butler his hat and gloves. "Good afternoon, Lady Symington." He kissed her cheek as she came near. "Though I do believe that he is *your* brother also."

His sister looked back at him steadily. "He is, though I

confess that I am becoming a little concerned for him. He is often foolish these days."

Peter let his lips curve into a small smile. "Yes, he is."

"And he has not always been so."

"No, he has not." Stifling a sigh, he looked back into her eyes. "But pray, what can I do in this vexing concern? I have beseeched him with my disapproval of his excessive indulgence, yet he dismisses my counsel with indifference."

"Then I shall speak with him."

"I do not think that it will do any good," Peter replied, gesturing for her to join him as they walked to the drawing room. "I do hope Lord Symington has not been too frustrated with my absence?" At the time of his brother's message, Peter had been discussing a business proposal with Viscount Symington, his sister's husband, and all had been going well. Had it been unwise of him to depart so hastily in order to help his brother not do anything foolish?

"No, you will find my husband enjoying your very fine French brandy," his sister told him, a quiet laugh in her voice. "Symington is patient to a fault."

"A trait I am very grateful for, given the circumstances," Peter replied, gesturing for the footmen to open the door for them both to step inside. "Thank you for understanding, Julia."

"But of course." Letting out a small sigh, she looked up at him, her eyes holding a good deal of concern as she gazed into his face. "Is it seemly for me to harbour such apprehension for our brother, or am I behaving as a foolish, overly anxious sister?"

Peter could not answer her, finding his own heart still uncertain. "I do not know," he offered, honestly. "Let us pray that he sees good sense... and that he sees it soon."

***

I do not know why, but there is something familiar about that young lady.

Peter frowned, his eyes fixing to a dark haired young woman who was standing with a lady he also vaguely recognized. He could not say why, could not understand why his mind tugged to her but there was something about her that seemed recognizable to him.

20

"Now, who is it that you are staring at?"

Peter started, then rolled his eyes as Lord Symington leaned in towards him, a knowing smile on his face. "I am not staring at anyone in particular."

"That young lady, is it?"

Without meaning to, Peter glanced towards the dark haired young lady again and Lord Symington immediately chuckled, making Peter's irritation burn.

"It is not that I am studying her for any other reason but I find her familiar... though I do not know why."

"Is it because she has caught your eye, mayhap?"

Peter quickly shook his head. "Not in the least."

"Then why?"

"Because... because she is familiar to me, though I do not know her name nor truly recognise her, if that makes sense to your ears?" Peter tried to explain but found himself failing. "It seems strange to me that I would see her face as recognisable but not know her title."

"Mayhap you have merely passed her in the street and taken note of her beauty."

Peter let out a heavy sigh, though his brother-in-law only grinned. "I do not have any interest in any young lady at present, whether they be beautiful or not."

Lord Symington tilted his head. "Do you not think that young lady – the one you have been watching – could be considered beautiful?"

Having no wish for Lord Symington to mock him any further, Peter gave her only a cursory glance before shrugging his shoulders. "She has fine features, certainly, but she does not speak to anyone. She simply stands there, silently, while the lady with her speaks to the two ladies with them."

Lord Symington frowned. "Why should such a thing matter?"

"Because it is clear she either has no interest in what is being spoken of – in which case, I might consider her a little rude – or she has no confidence to join in the conversation, which I might then consider to be a lack of character. All this is to say that yes, whether she be beautiful or not, I would not even think to consider her."

"I see." His friend smiled suddenly, making Peter frown at

21

the response. "It is interesting to me that you are doing your level best to claim that you have no interest – and *could* have no interest – in the lady whatsoever. Are you quite certain that you do not find her at all intriguing?"

"Only because I do not know why I find her familiar, that is all." Speaking crisply, Peter looked back at his friend. "I am here to enjoy the Season, as you are."

"Ah but there is a difference between you and I."

Peter frowned. "Namely?"

"That I am wed and you are not." Lord Symington chuckled. "Therefore, I can truly enjoy the Season for what it is while you must continually be considering the young ladies around you and wondering whether or not any of them will be suitable enough for you."

Shaking his head, Peter let out a low chuckle. "I can assure you, I have no intention of doing any such thing. When I marry – and yes, I am aware that I must marry in order to produce the heir – it will be by arrangement only. Mayhap a second cousin or the like. Someone who will be entirely suitable."

Lord Symington lifted an eyebrow. "And you will not permit your heart to say anything in that regard?"

"Certainly, I will not!" Peter scoffed. "I do not think that any gentleman who has any wisdom would permit their heart to have any sort of say in who they marry. That would be foolishness, surely, given that one's heart can be so fickle."

There came a long silence and as Peter looked back at his friend, he realized with agonizing slowness, that he had managed to insult him. Closing his eyes, he winced, letting out his breath in a hiss.

"I came to care for your sister before we ever considered engagement," Lord Symington said, quietly. "And I do not think that I lack wisdom."

"I would not suggest for a moment that you were in any way foolish," Peter said quickly, a flush of heat rising up his chest and into his face. "Forgive me, I did not think that through with any sense of true consideration."

"No, you did not," Lord Symington replied, a little dryly. "Though I shall forgive you, given that we are family."

Peter put one hand to his heart.

"And I should tell you that there is ample opportunity for any gentlemen of good standing *and* of wisdom to fall in love with a young lady," Lord Symington continued, firmly. "You ought not to shut yourself away from it."

With a small, wry smile, Peter shook his head. "That is not for me. I have no interest in allowing my heart to *feel* anything, not in that regard at least. It seems a good deal too tiring."

"Tiring?" Lord Symington laughed. "I can assure you, falling in love does nothing other than brings joy and happiness to my heart rather that fatiguing me. I have always been grateful for the day that I met your sister. It has brought me life!"

"And I am glad to hear that from you," Peter replied, firmly, "but I have always been practically minded and have no intention of allowing emotion to cloud my judgement."

All the same, when he turned his attention back towards the room at large, his gaze seemed to demand that he draw himself back to the young lady whom he recognized. He did all he could not to look at her but his gaze found him back there time and again to the point that, eventually, he turned himself away completely so he would not stare at the lady and wonder at her. Her memory continued to niggle at him and, desperate for relief, Peter went in search of a brandy and a game of cards, determined now to put the whole matter out of his mind.

Chapter Three

"Now, do stand tall and smile."

Anne looked at her aunt. "Smile? At whom?"

"At anyone – at everyone," came the reply. "You should always attempt to keep a light smile on your face for it adds to your countenance *and* catches the attention of those around you. You will, no doubt, soon have gentlemen and ladies seeking an introduction to you."

Anne smiled at this, albeit ruefully. "That is kind of you to say, Aunt, but I do not think that such a thing will be so. Gentlemen were always drawn to my younger sisters and whenever they drew near, I found myself so ill at ease, my words tripped over each other and I ended up falling into silence. Therefore, any gentleman or lady who *did* come to seek an introduction with me soon regretted it or, as my father told me, would have forgotten about me just as quickly."

"There you go again, you see?" Lady Mayhew clicked her tongue. "You are speaking about something your father has said, something that *he* has told you which I have told you already must be pushed out of your memory and be gone from your thoughts." She smiled quickly so that Anne would not take any offence. "I am not berating you, my dear. Instead, I am encouraging you to set the past behind you and to think on the present moment. I will guide you and, should you struggle in conversation, I will be present to make certain there is no embarrassment on your part or awareness of your struggle on the part of whomever you are speaking with. All will be well, I assure you."

Anne looked out across the growing crowd, her skin prickling as though she were somehow aware that someone out there was watching her. Pressing her lips together, she glanced from left to right, only for her gaze to snag on one particular gentleman who was standing a short distance away, his hands clasped tightly behind his back and his eyes searching hers. The moment after she looked at him again and smiled, the gentleman tore his gaze away and, a short time thereafter, turned around entirely. Anne, a little nonplussed, dropped her own gaze to her clasped hands, a little unsure as to what had taken place between them. Had she ought not to smile? Her aunt had only just instructed her to always smile and yet here she was, attempting to do that very thing only for the gentleman to turn himself away quickly. There was something familiar about him, she considered, studying him with another few, quick glances in his direction though she never allowed herself to linger long for fear that he would see her looking at him. He had thick, dark hair which swept across his forehead, a tight, square jaw and eyes that flashed as though he were thinking about something very serious indeed. Anne still could not understand how she knew his face and yet that very same face settled in her mind with an awareness that she had seen him somewhere before.

"Now, there is an excellent gentleman to be introduced to."

Reluctantly, Anne pulled her attention away from the gentleman and looked to where her aunt was gesturing.

"Lord Foley," Lady Mayhew continued, nodding in the gentleman's direction. "He is a good sort though he still has not taken a wife. I believe he wants to take on as much of society as he can before he chooses to wed."

Anne glanced at her aunt, aware of the buzzing in her mind. "And you think that he is a good sort?"

Lady Mayhew nodded. "Yes, of course I do. He is not a gentleman that gambles or the like. He is not a rogue nor a scoundrel. He is unwed, yes but that has not encouraged him towards debauchery or the like. From what I have heard, he has a very fine character and has never treated anyone poorly."

"That is good, then."

Her aunt turned to her, regarding Anne carefully. "You wish to be introduced to him?"

"I – I will do whatever you think best for me," Anne replied, hearing the catch of worry in her voice but refusing to permit it to grab hold of her. She had spent the entirety of the afternoon forcing herself not to give in to her worry, not to let it tighten a noose around her neck.

With a smile on her face, Lady Mayhew squeezed her hand. "I know this takes a great deal of strength for you, my dear, but it will be good for you to do, I promise. Come with me."

Anne willed her feet forward, tension spiraling through her, her stomach clenching hard as she went with her aunt. Her mind recalled the many times she had been unable to form even a single sentence such had been her worry and her awareness of her father's heavy eye upon her.

Lady Mayhew has promised me that it shall be different this time," she reminded herself, silently as Lady Mayhew led her towards the mysterious gentleman. *I must trust her judgement.*

"Good *evening,* Lord Folley. How good to see you again."

"Lady Mayhew!" Lorrd Folley exclaimed, grasping Lady Mayhew's hand and pressing it as though she were a dear friend he had not seen in some time. "How lovely it is to see you again. Do tell me that your husband is with you in London? It has been much too long since he and I have had a conversation about the current state of politics!"

Lady Mayhew laughed as Anne forced herself to keep her chin up, though she could not quite make herself look into Lord Folley's face. He spoke with such warmth and confidence, she felt herself shrinking back within herself, sure that she would make a fool of herself should she even attempt to open her mouth.

"Alas, he has not joined me as yet but he shall soon," Lady Mayhew replied, turning to Anne. "Might I present Miss Anne Jennings to you, however?"

"Miss Jennings!" Lord Folley exclaimed, as though she were yet another old friend he had yet to reacquaint himself with. "How delighted I am to meet you. Are you related to Lady Mayhew or a friend of this wonderful lady?"

Anne swallowed quickly, her mouth dry. "I am her niece." The words came out in a barely audible voice but she had managed to speak them nonetheless – and Lord Folley's enthusiasm covered over her embarrassment at how poorly she had spoken.

"Her niece? Goodness, how wonderful it is to be acquainted with you, then! Lady Mayhew, how lovely it must be for you to be able to chaperone your niece this Season."

"It is very lovely indeed," Lady Mayhew replied, warmly, though Anne caught the twinkle in her eyes as she glanced at her. Mayhap she was all too aware of just how overwhelming Lord Folley's effusiveness could be. "And are you enjoying the Season thus far?"

Lord Folley nodded enthusiastically, his fair hair falling into his eyes though he quickly brushed it back. "Very much indeed. Though I can see that your dance card is hanging on your wrist,

Miss Jennings, and that as yet, I have not written my name upon it! That must be remedied at once!"

Panic instantly grasped Anne's heart though she did as he had asked her and managed to pull her dance card from her wrist and thereafter, hand it to him – albeit with trembling fingers. She dared not look at either her aunt or at the gentleman, gazing down at the floor and taking in long, slow breaths as she fought to contain her worry. When was the last time she had stepped out with a gentleman? She could barely remember and though her aunt had aided her by way of providing her with a dancing master to go over all of the dances, Anne's fear grew so large, she felt her heart twisting with fright. In her mind, all she saw were the various scenarios where she herself tumbled to the floor, having either tangled her feet with Lord Folley's, or taken a foolish misstep and ruined the dance entirely.

"The cotillion, I think." Lord Folley handed the dance card back to Anne who dutifully took it, managing to murmur a thank you as she placed the ribbon back over her wrist. "Yes, I think that shall suit me very well indeed. I have not danced the cotillion since last Season and – "

Before he could conclude his sentence, a weighty force collided with Anne, causing her to lose her breath. At the very same time, something tore down her heel and she let out a cry of pain, falling forward, her whole body tumbling of its own accord, unable to right itself. Strong arms caught her, with Lord Folley's harsh voice filling the air as a buzzing settled in Anne's ears. Blinking furiously, she tried to stand though her foot pained her a great deal.

"Goodness, are you quite all right?" Lady Mayhew caught Anne's hand, her eyes wide with shock as Lord Folley's strong arms held Anne tight, making sure she stayed upright and clearly aware that she still needed his support. "That insufferable dolt collided with you, completely without any semblance of propriety!"

"Get to your feet!" Lord Folley released Anne gently, one hand gesturing wildly to the gentleman who, Anne noticed, was lying on the floor though he was laughing uproariously, as though what had just happened was nothing short of mirthful. "How dare you injure this lady with your foolishness?"

Anne, now leaning on Lady Mayhew, could only watch as the

27

fair haired gentleman slowly pushed himself up to his hands and knees, shaking his head as laughter still came from him. Pain shot up into her leg and, turning her head, she looked down to see her slipper quite squashed. "My foot is very sore, Aunt," she whispered, still clinging onto her aunt's arm with one hand. "I fear I may have to sit down and rest."

"Of course." Lady Mayhew looked to Lord Folley. "Might you aid me in bringing Miss Jennings to a parlour or some other place she can sit?"

"Yes, indeed." Lord Folley stepped forward and, rather than taking Anne's arm, grasped the arm of the gentleman who was struggling to stand and hauled him to his feet. "Though whoever *this* fellow is ought first to apologise."

Anne's stomach twisted, shock rippling across her chest. This gentleman was the very same as the one she had observed falling out of the carriage as he had attempted to climb back in some days ago. From the swift catch of breath from her aunt, Anne believed that she recognized him also.

"Apologise for what?" the gentleman asked, swaying back and forth as he grinned inanely. "I fell, that is all."

"You fell into Miss Jennings and have injured her!" Lord Folley exclaimed, as the gentleman shrugged. "Your foolishness has caused her pain!"

"I did not see her." The gentleman sniffed, his smile slipping. "There was no deliberate act here."

"All the same, you should apologise," Lord Folley said angrily, his eyebrows knotting together. "This lady is bearing a great deal of pain because of your actions."

Anne waited and watched but the gentleman who had fallen into her seemed to give very little consideration to what she had suffered by his hand. Her shoulders dropped, her face coloring as she realized just how many people were now looking at her, observing the exchange and seeing what had happened.

It seemed her first ball was not to be as quiet as she had hoped.

Chapter Four

"Look, there is some altercation there."

Peter lifted an eyebrow. "In the ballroom?"

"Yes, in the ballroom." Lord Telford, one of Peter's friends whom he had been speaking with for the last few minutes, gestured across the ballroom. "Look, there are two gentlemen standing arguing with one another. And a small band of gentlemen and ladies are now watching."

Peter narrowed his eyes, a thudding of his heart beginning to speak of the dread which immediately began to fill him. "Please let it not be Henley."

"Your brother?"

Nodding, Peter glanced at his friend and then looked back at the scene unfolding some distance away. "Yes. I am afraid that my brother has become something of a lawless fellow, seeking to do whatever he pleases and whatever he wishes without any sort of immediate consideration as to what the consequences will be."

"Oh." Lord Telford frowned. "That may stain your reputation also, if you are not careful."

A scowl pulled at Peter's features. "I am doing my level best to pull him back from himself," he stated, firmly. "I do try to tug him away and I always come to his aid when he sends for it but no matter what I say or what I do, he is not in the least bit interest in doing anything other than what he himself pleases."

"I see." Lord Telford shook his head and sighed. "That must be difficult for you."

"It is." Peter's scowl grew. "But I am only grateful that my sister has married already. It is her reputation that I would fear for the most." As he spoke, he caught sight of Lord Symington's face, seeing how he made his way towards Peter and Lord Telford and instantly, the dread in his heart grew.

"Symington?" Moving forward, Peter saw the worry in his brother-in-law's face. "What is going on?"

"It is your brother."

Peter instantly closed his eyes. "What is it that he has done?"

Lord Symington jerked his head in the direction of the

ongoing altercation. "Come quickly, if you please. Lord Henley will not apologise to the lady and I am afraid that he will soon do something even more foolish."

"What happened?" Peter asked again, throwing an apologetic glance towards Lord Telford though he hurried after Lord Symington. "What did my brother do?"

"Injured a young lady."

Peter's heart lurched, his gut twisting. Whatever had his brother done such a foolish thing for? It was one thing to distress a gentleman or two but quite another to pain a lady! And to then to refuse to apologise for it? Whatever was his brother thinking?

"Here." Lord Symington stopped and then beckoned Peter forward. "There are many listening now. The *ton* will be speaking of this tomorrow."

Recognizing the shame that would be brought to his family name should he not attempt to resolve this, Peter took in a deep breath, lifted his chin and stepped forward, coming to stand between his brother and a gentleman he vaguely recognized.

"Whatever is going on?" he asked, keeping his voice filled with as much confidence as he dared. "What has happened, Henley?"

His brother shrugged. "I fell."

"Lord Denfield, is it not?"

The other gentleman spoke and Peter turned his attention to him at once. "It is, though you must forgive me for I have quite forgotten your title."

The gentleman drew himself up, his mouth a thin line, a pinched expression across his eyes. "Lord Folley."

"Yes, of course." Recognition swept over Peter at once. "I saw the commotion and thought it best to come and join you all. Might I ask what has taken place?"

Lord Folley threw out one arm to the young lady standing to his left. She was leaning heavily on the arm of an older woman and Peter quickly recognized her as the young lady whom he had been considering earlier that evening. Whatever had happened to her?

"You may as well ask Miss Jennings," Lord Folley told him, harshly, "since *she* is the one now injured."

"Injured?" Peter's eyebrows shot up, then he looked to his brother who, much to his embarrassment, merely shrugged. "I am terribly sorry." He looked back to the young lady again. "Miss Jennings, might I ask what happened?"

The lady's eyes went to her chaperone and after receiving a small nod from her, she began to speak though her voice quavered terribly – no doubt, Peter considered, from the shock of what had taken place. Fully aware of the small crowd watching and mortified already at his brother's behavior – even without knowing the full extent of it – Peter gave the lady his full attention.

"I was speaking with Lord Folley here," the lady began, looking to the gentleman who nodded fervently, "with my aunt, Lady Mayhew, here to the other side of me. All of a sudden, I felt a great pain at the back of my foot and I was thrown forward."

"Had not Lord Folley acted so swiftly, she would have fallen to the floor and sustained who knows what sort of injuries!" Lady Mayhew exclaimed, her face red with clear upset. "My niece cannot even walk without support given the injury to her foot!"

Peter closed his eyes. "How dreadful," he replied, truthfully, hot with shame over his brother's lack of consideration. "And Lord Henley – my brother – was the one who knocked into you so?"

"He was." It was Lord Folley who spoke rather than the lady herself, though she did not appear to be at all frustrated that he had done so for her gaze cast to his and then she looked away again, her face still pale. "And then when I demanded that he make his apology to the lady, he would not! He stated it had not been done purposefully so, therefore, there was no requirement for him to speak so!"

Peter looked to his brother who, much to his disgust, was now standing with a slight smile hovering about his lips, his hands on his hips though he still swayed a little. What was he to do? The lady was clearly hurt and upset by what Lord Henley had done and yet his brother stood there, smiling and mocking as though this was something that she ought to have expected from him.

"Henley." Peter frowned hard, seeing his brother look at him lazily. "The lady is owed a sincere apology." He felt like a parent chiding their young son and that only added to his embarrassment, through his brother seemed to care very little for that, given the way he shrugged.

"I apologise, Miss Jennings." Lord Henley let his hands fall to his sides and then turned away. "I do hope you recover soon."

There was no genuineness in Lord Henley's words and Peter wanted to grab his brother by the lapels and shake him, hard, but all he could do – as every other person watching did – was to gaze at him as he staggered away, lurching forward as he made for the door. Peter could only pray that his brother was about to make his way home rather than go to Whites or to a gambling den but his heart told him that Henley would, no doubt, make his way to a place where he could imbibe a little more and laugh a little harder.

Which meant that the responsibility to apologise profusely to Miss Jennings now fell to him.

"I can only apologise, Miss Jennings." Peter turned and walked directly towards the lady, seeing how her gaze darted away from his face – no doubt because of the upset that she felt at present over his brother's actions. "First I apologise for what happened and secondly, I apologise for my brother's lack of sincerity. He is clearly in his cups and I am certain that, once he has returned to himself, he will be highly embarrassed at his own behaviour and will beg to apologise to you again, though with a good deal more sincerity this time." Bowing, he put one hand to his heart. "It is a poor apology coming from me, I know, but it is all I can do. I am truly sorry for what you have endured, Miss Jennings. There is no excuse for my brother's actions and I am ashamed of him."

Miss Jennings' eyes went to his and for a moment, all of Peter's breath left his body at the vivid green he saw there. Her eyes were startling, bright and deep, in stark contrast to the paleness of her cheeks. But then, she pulled her gaze away and he could finally take his breath again, closing his eyes for a moment so he might recollect himself.

"It is better than no apology at all, at least." Lady Mayhew sniffed, looking to her niece again, her expression filled with concern. "Now, my dear, you have been standing too long. We need to make certain that you sit down and rest that foot. I shall have to take a look at it. It shall certainly be bruised."

Peter winced. "I should like to aid you to the parlour, if I can."

"There is no need." Lord Folley pushed forward, coming to stand again by Miss Jennings. "The lady does not require your aid. *I* shall take the lady away from both yourself and from your brother.

There has been a great injury done this evening and the last thing Miss Jennings requires is more of your company." Turning his back on Peter, Lord Folley took Miss Jennings' arm and as Peter watched, shame mounting, both Lady Mayhew and he led Miss Jennings away. She was limping dreadfully and Peter closed his eyes, his whole being burning with the disgrace of what his brother had done and the dark shadow he had flung across the family name.

Peter was going to have to do something about it. Henley could not be permitted to continue, not when there was more than just his own reputation at stake.

***

"I have had enough, Henley!"

Peter marched up and down the drawing room as both his brother, sister and brother-in-law sat watching him, though out of the three, Lord Henley appeared to be the least concerned. Indeed, as Peter returned his gaze to him, Henley yawned widely and made no attempt whatsoever to hide it.

"Do you not understand what has happened?" Peter asked, throwing up his hands as his brother observed him without any appearance of concern. "You injured Miss Jennings! I have had news this morning that the heel of her foot was left raw and bleeding and that her ankle has significant bruises, given the way it twisted as she fell. You are responsible for all of that, Henley!"

His brother shrugged. "It was not deliberate."

"But all the same, *you* are responsible," Peter said again, as his sister nodded, though Lord Symington merely ran one hand over his chin, watching the conversation rather than taking part in it. "In your inebriated state, you injured the lady and now she is under the doctor's care."

"Why does such a thing matter?" Henley asked, sounding exasperated that Peter was bringing up this in conversation. "I apologised to the lady, did I not?"

"You did not," their sister interrupted, her eyebrows lifting high. "I was not present but I have already heard how Lord Folley demanded that you apologise for injuring the lady and you refused. Do you not see how the gossip about this is already spreading around London?"

Lord Henley merely looked away from her, his jaw tightening.

"It is bringing disgrace," Lord Symington murmured, though Henley instantly rolled his eyes. "*You* are bringing disgrace, not only to your name but also to the name of your brother and to mine also!"

"I do not see how."

"Because," Peter explained, throwing up his hands, "you are our brother. Your disgrace touches both my reputation and the reputation of Symington because he is wed to our sister. Do not pretend that you do not understand, Henley. I know that you do, it is simply that you do not want to listen to us."

A small quirk touched his brother's lips. "Finally, you understand," he replied, as Peter's anger began to burn. "I do not want to listen to you and nor do I want to change my behaviour in any way. I am perfectly contented in living as I please and in whatever manner I choose. I do not need you all to tell me to change my situation just to please you both."

Peter closed his eyes, horrified by his brother's selfishness. "Then you do not care about your sister or I."

"It is not that I do not care," came the reply. "It is only that I do not think that what you are saying is particularly relevant *or* that it holds the strength that you state. I am sure that Miss Jennings will soon recover, the gossip mongers will find something more to speak of and I will be left to continue on with my life just as I please."

Dropping his head forward, Peter let out a groan of frustration and sank down into a chair. He had done his best to speak to his brother, to make it clear to him what it was that he had done and why it was causing such trouble but it seemed that no matter what he said, Lord Henley was going to ignore him entirely.

"Brother, please do consider what we are saying to you." Julia spoke quietly, though the fervency of her voice was still present. "It is not fair of you to ignore us entirely. I do not want to bear any disgrace or have any dirt placed upon my reputation but I cannot prevent that, unfortunately, given that it is entirely in *your* hands."

Silence reigned and Peter lifted his head, a faint hope beginning to build in his heart as he saw his brother frown.

"Please," Julia continued, softly. "Might you not think about what the continuation of such behavior will do to us, Henley? What if the children I hope to bear Lord Symington one day are looked down upon because they are *your* nephew or niece? Are you truly contented with that?"

"I do not want to be told how I must live!" Lord Henley got to his feet suddenly, striding across the room. "You are insisting that I behave in a particular manner and I have no desire to do so."

"We are asking you to consider how much you imbibe and the behaviours which come thereafter, yes," Peter admitted. "I do not think that is such a dreadful thing for you to consider."

"Well, I do."

Peter let out a sigh of breath rather than say anything more, for his brother was clearly without any willingness to even listen to them.

"Then I do not think that you can ask Denfield for any further help."

Peter turned his attention to Lord Symington, seeing him spread out his hands as he continued. "How can you beg your brother to come to your aid, to save you from whatever perplexity you've twisted yourself into, and then refuse to listen to him – to even acknowledge him – when he tells you that your behaviour is causing injury not only to yourself but also to him? And also to Juila and myself?"

Watching his brother, Peter saw Henley frown. "But I require his aid."

"And he requires you to reign yourself in a little." Lord Symington arched an eyebrow. "What is it that you will say to this, Henley? I am sure that Denfield agrees with me that this cannot continue."

"I do." Peter shook his head and his brother looked at him. "I do not want to continue to come at your every beck and call, brother. Not if it means that, when I come to you with my concerns, you ignore them." A knot tied itself in his stomach, fearing what would happen should he refuse to go to his brother's aid when next he called, but he realized that Lord Symington was right. Henley had to realize that this expectation could not be something that continued without any alteration.

"Then... then I do not require your help." Lord Henley lifted his chin. "This is ridiculous. I did not do anything wrong. I – "

"You knocked a young lady to the ground!" Peter found himself on his feet, his hands balling into fists. "You injured her foot so badly, she could not walk from the ballroom without *two* people supporting her! She will not be able to dance for some days, if not weeks! Had Lord Folley not caught her, she would have crumpled to the floor – and most likely, you would have fallen on top of her – and caused even more injury! How can you say now that you did nothing wrong? You are the *only* one at fault here!"

His words echoed around the room, bouncing off the walls as he narrowed his gaze, his breathing ragged as he fixed his gaze to his brother, seeing how Lord Henley's eyes had widened and, as Peter took a step closer, how he took a step back.

"You are the only one at fault," Peter repeated, his voice hoarse now such was his anger. "What is worse, what is all the more shameful, is that you did not even think to apologise. You mocked the entire situation and those who saw it, those who witnessed it, now think very poorly of you. Your reputation is slowly being torn to shreds, piece by piece... and it is done by your very own hands."

Lord Henley blinked furiously, his mouth opening and shutting but Peter felt himself weary of the entire situation. Swinging around, he made for the door, hearing his sister call his name but giving her not even a cursory glance. Instead, he stepped out into the hallway and strode down it, having no thought as to where he was going. The only thing he wanted was to get away from his arrogant, selfish brother before his anger grew to such heights, it could not be drawn back under his control.

I shall write to Miss Jennings and apologise again, he told himself, his breathing still much too quick and fast. *And I shall have to pray that, somehow, Henley sees sense and returns to the quiet, reformed gentleman he was before.*

36

Chapter Five

"How is your foot today, my dear?"

Anne smiled warmly as her aunt came into the drawing room. "It is much improved, Aunt."

"Can you stand?" Lady Mayhew frowned as Anne nodded fervently. "Can you walk?"

"Yes, but with a slight limp," Anne answered, truthfully. "And there is a little pain still but it is bearable."

Lady Mayhew clicked her tongue. "You should not walk too far. It will only add to your pain, I am sure." Sitting down opposite, she looked Anne straight in the eye. "And has Lord Henley written to you?"

Anne shook her head.

"That is an absolute disgrace," Lady Mayhew exclaimed, getting up again almost immediately and beginning to pace around the room. "I do not know the gentleman at all but what I have *seen* of his behaviour and character, I am sure that he is not an excellent gentleman at all."

"I do not think he can be." Now that she was recovered, Anne was able to look back on the incident without concern, recalling how Lord Henley had merely shrugged and then turned away rather than apologizing. "Lord Folley was excellent in his defence of me, however."

"Yes, he was." Lady Mayhew sighed and clasped her hands in her lap. "If only he were a gentleman willing to consider matrimony! I would have urged him towards you otherwise."

Anne offered her aunt a small smile but said nothing more. Lord Folley *was*, of course, an excellent fellow and she was truly glad for everything that he had done in coming to her aid but there was nothing there of interest when it came to her consideration of him. She saw him as an amiable fellow, someone she would be glad to speak with – and dance with – should he ask her permission but there was no flicker of interest in her heart.

"Lord Denfield has written you a very pretty apology, however," Lady Mayhew sighed, looking at the letter which Anne now had on the table to her right. "That is something, at least, though I should have preferred Lord Henley to come and speak with you himself. He was the one who injured you, after all."

"Yes, he was but I do not think he will appear." Anne smiled and, in doing so, took some of the heavy clouds from her aunt's expression. "But I shall be grateful that the *ton* has not thought badly of me in all of this and has, in fact, been nothing but a support."

Lady Mayhew smiled back at her. "That is true, I suppose, though it is to be expected. Lord Folley's enthusiasm to tell everyone about what took place has helped that a great deal, though of course, you deserve every word spoken in your defence."

"I am sure I shall be fully recovered very soon, Aunt," Anne replied, quickly. "We are to go to a soiree tomorrow evening, are we not?"

Her aunt nodded though there came a flash of worry into her eyes at the very same time. "We are but I can send our apologies if you do not wish to attend."

"No, I very much wish to go," Anne replied, quickly. Having been resting – first, in bed and secondly, on the couch in the drawing room for the last few days, she felt herself almost desperate to be out of the townhouse and out in society. It was not that she had gained any confidence in her days resting, however, there was not an urge to fling herself back into society for the sake of it but rather because she found herself a little bored. Her aunt had talked at length about what had happened and Anne had done nothing other than listen and murmur on occasion. She had read sometimes, taken up her needlework but still, nothing seemed to encourage her in the way the thought of returning to society did. Perhaps being with her aunt was filling her with a renewed confidence already!

"Then so long as you are careful and do not dance or the like, for no doubt, as the evening wears on, some young gentleman will mention dancing."

Anne, who had not yet stood up with any gentleman given what had happened to her, gave her aunt a wry smile. "I give you my word, I will not dance."

"And you will rest," Lady Mayhew continued, quickly, as Anne's nod grew all the more fervent. "You will sit down as much as you can."

"I promise I shall."

"Good." The worry did not leave her aunt's expression as she regarded Anne. "Are you sure you are going to be well enough recovered?"

"I am," Anne promised, just as a scratch came at the door and, after a moment, a footman stepped in with a note. Anne watched as her aunt read it, saw how her eyebrows lifted, only for her to nod fervently and, thereafter, glance at Anne herself.

"Lord Henley writes to ask if you will be present at the soiree for he is well acquainted with Lord and Lady Applecross and they have evidently told him you are to be attending."

"Lord Henley wrote me a note?" Anne repeated, reaching out for the letter which was then passed to her. "Simply to ask that?"

"He asked me, in fact, which is very proper," Lady Mayhew replied, though she did not smile as the paper was handed to Anne. "I do not know what I think about this."

Anne quickly read the note, taking in everything it said. "It states that he hopes I will be present so that he might apologise to me properly."

"It does."

Looking back at her aunt, Anne pointed to the letter. "Is this not what we hoped for? What we wanted?"

"It is but to do so publicly is a little... uncouth. I would have preferred him to come to this house and apologise to you here, in front of me."

"But nothing will happen," Anne said, quickly, seeing how the worry on her aunt's face lined it all the more. "You know that I will be very safe beside you and since I am to be sitting and resting, it is not as though he can knock into me again!"

This brought a small smile to Lady Mayhew's face and she nodded slowly before handing the note back to the footman. "Have a returned message spoken to Lord Henley, informing him that we hope to be present. That is all that is to be said."

The footman nodded and quit the room, leaving Anne to study her aunt's tight expression. It was clear that she did not approve of Lord Henley in any way whatsoever – and Anne herself could not blame her. Lord Henley had been both ill-mannered and discourteous and even now, the thought of seeing him again, of

39

speaking with him meant that her whole frame tightened at the thought. It was not a pleasant sensation.

"I am sure all will go well," she said, seeing her aunt's gaze return to her own. "There will be nothing to fear and, mayhap, we will gain the apology we hope for and all will be well again."

***

"I am sorry to hear that you are still recovering."

Anne managed a smile, finding herself rather overwhelmed with the sheer number of people who had come to speak with her. Evidently, news of what had taken place at the ball had made its way round society rather quickly and everyone now appeared to be very concerned indeed. "I will be dancing again soon, I am sure." She did not know what else to say, her fingers tingling as she squeezed her hands into tight fists, forcing herself to remain just as she was with the smile pinned to her face.

"All the same, it is a great disgrace that Lord Henley would not apologise," a young lady said, coming to sit beside Anne rather than standing, as the other two gentlemen and one lady were doing. "I think I would have been quite furious with him, had I been in your position."

Anne looked surreptitiously around for her aunt but Lady Mayhew was nowhere to be seen, perhaps thinking that Anne would be quite safe now that she was safely ensconced in a corner of the room on a comfortable sofa.

"I would have been too," another young lady said, her eyes wide. "I fear I may have snubbed him outright!"

"Indeed, it is no gentleman who refuses to apologise for his mistake," one of the gentlemen added, making the two young ladies nod in fervent agreement. "It is utterly disgraceful. If I had been in attendance, I would have administered a stern rebuke to him instead!" This was said with a triumphant smile, though Anne shuddered at the thought of this gentleman reprimanding Lord Henley. To her mind, that would only have added to the difficulties rather than aiding it in any way.

"Come now, let me fetch you something to drink, Miss Jennings." The second gentleman smiled and bent himself a little towards her, a smile on his face. "Some wine, perhaps?"

40

"Yes, please." Anne did feel herself a little parched but at the same time, thought that having something in her hand from which she could sip might help her not to have to find answers to questions she did not want in the first place. "That is very kind of you." She could not remember the gentleman's name – could not remember any of her new acquaintances' titles – and forced the corners of her mouth to lift up and stay there so she might appear contented with their prolonged company rather than being worried about it.

"You must be so very upset with all that has taken place," said one of the ladies, though the one sitting next to her leaned closer and then shooed the speaker back, as though she were protecting Anne in some way.

"We are asking Miss Jennings a good too many questions, I think," she said, crisply. "If she *is* upset, as we all believe, then what good will it be for us to ask her of her emotions at present? It will do no good whatsoever."

Anne took in a breath and offered the lady beside her a small smile, grateful, in fact, for her interruption. The young lady smiled and gave Anne a tiny nod, perhaps aware that this was exactly what Anne had been looking for by way of support.

"In fact, I think we should all stop questioning her for it must be quite overwhelming," the young lady continued, with a good deal more confidence than Anne could ever have projected. "Let us speak of something else, mayhap?"

"I am sure that Miss Jennings can speak for herself rather than require *your* aid," one of the young ladies snapped, her eyes sharpening. "You have no need to project yourself in such a way, Lady Grace."

Anne's throat tightened as she caught every person looking at her again, aware now that they all expected her to say something, either by way of supporting Lady Grace or to encourage them all to ignore her. "I – I do feel a little fatigued."

"You see?" Lady Grace waved her hand again, as though to push every gentleman and lady back. "Enough questions, now."

Much to Anne's relief, the young ladies appeared rather disappointed that Anne was not going to say anything more and stepped away at once, leaving only the gentlemen. The one who had gone to fetch her a drink returned with it and smiled graciously upon handing it to her, only to then be tugged away by *another* young lady who pleaded with him to come to join her in conversation. The last gentleman then took his leave of her also and Anne let out a slow breath of relief, her eyes closing briefly.

"I do hope you are not upset by the fact that everyone has taken their leave so quickly."

With a shake of her head, Anne smiled at Lady Grace. "Indeed not. I am rather relieved, I confess it."

"I should apologise for my own fervency." Lady Grace's green eyes snapped with obvious frustration. "I always tell myself that I have no need to incline myself towards gossip but I find that I am very inclined towards it regardless."

"I understand that it is a part of society that one must be open to."

"Mayhap," Lady Grace replied, sighing, "but it is not a good part of society, I confess. Which is why I ought to be avoiding it rather than pursuing it!"

Finding Lady Grace to be warm and companionable, Anne found herself relaxing in her company. She had not often had a friend during her time in the London Season previously for she had always been in company with her sisters but she certainly would appreciate one now.

"Might I ask if this is your first Season?"

Lady Grace trilled a laugh and shook her head. "No, it is not. It is my third! My father is most insistent that I find a match this Season though I myself am not at all inclined towards matrimony. I think I should prefer to be a spinster and make my own way in life."

Anne, who had often thought of spinsterhood to be a very dreadful thing indeed, quickly shook her head. "I do not believe that being a spinster would permit for a great deal of freedom. There would be financial difficulty and that would bring its own sorrows."

"Yes, that it true, I suppose." Lady Grace offered her a wry smile. "It is only that I want very much to be able to make my own choices and decisions and thus far, I have been able to make very few! Though I have refused to marry three gentlemen that my father has suggested."

Anne's eyes widened in surprise at how wonderfully

confident this young lady seemed to be. Had she been offered even one gentleman to consider, then she would have done so without question!

"Miss Jennings?"

Her surprise grew all the more as a deep voice caught her attention, leaving her to stare into the face of none other than Lord Denfield. He bowed though his mouth was pulled into a firm line, his dark blue eyes holding fast to hers when he lifted his head.

"Good evening, Lord Denfield," Anne murmured, her heart leaping about in her chest. "I did not expect – "

"My brother was meant to be here this evening and, more than that, was meant to apologise to you," Lord Denfield began, interrupting her though he did not seem to notice he had done so, most likely because her voice was so quiet. "He has been unable to make it, however."

Anne blinked. "Oh."

"I did not want you to be sitting here in expectation, waiting for his arrival," the gentleman continued, rubbing one hand over his chin, though Anne was sure that the spark in his eyes spoke of frustration. "Another time, I am sure."

"Of course." There was nothing else for her to say, nothing to be responded to for she certainly was not about to make a fuss, was not going to complain that Lord Henley ought to be here. "Thank you for informing me."

Lord Denfield nodded and without a word, walked away from both Anne and Lady Grace without so much as a glance or a nod in Lady Grace's direction.

"Goodness, is that Lord Denfield?"

Anne nodded. "Yes. His brother, Lord Henley, who injured me so was meant to be here this evening. Evidently, he is no longer able to attend."

"Or did not wish to," Lady Grace remarked, with a slightly wry smile. "Perhaps he wishes to apologise in private so that fewer people will watch him as he does so."

With a small shrug, Anne watched Lord Denfield walk away, her heart beginning to feel heavy and weighted in her chest. "Or mayhap Lord Henley does not wish to apologise at all."

44

Chapter Six

She really is rather beautiful.

Peter scowled to himself as the thought came into his mind. He did not much like it, did not much want it and thus, he discarded it just as quickly as he could.

"You are looking at Miss Jennings, I see."

Peter smiled as his sister arched an eyebrow. "I am. It is because I am wondering how long it shall be before Henley offers her the apology she is owed."

Julia shook her head and sighed. "You have spoken to him twice already and he still refuses to do as he ought. It has been almost a fortnight since the incident took place and though the *ton* might have forgotten a little of what happened, I certainly have not. I continue to press him, to beg him to apologise to her but he will not."

Peter frowned. "What does he say when you ask him to apologise?"

His sister let out another heavy breath. "He states that he has no need to do so – or that he will do so in his own time."

"In his on time," Peter repeated, his words scathing. "That means that he shall never do it."

"Mayhap it does." Julia sighed heavily, slipping her arm through Peter's as they continued to meander through Hyde Park, leaving Miss Jennings and her friend to talk and laugh together, all without noticing Peter's approach. The fashionable hour was always busy and Peter had spied Miss Jennings without having had any intention of searching for her but it seemed that fate had every intention of reminding him of his present struggle with his brother. "Where is Henley this afternoon? I thought he was to join us in the park?"

Peter scowled darkly. "Our gracious brother has decided to take himself to Lord Grigson's house for the afternoon."

"Lord Grigson?" Julia's voice was filled with alarm which Peter could understand, given the reputation of the gentleman. "That is not a good connection to foster."

"And yet, he will do so regardless." Peter's jaw tightened all the more, frustrated over how little progress he appeared to be making with his brother. "I have tried and I have failed when it comes to Miss Jennings *and* his continuing foolish behaviour which merits no respect whatsoever. It all falls on deaf ears. He has no interest in listening to me, has no desire to pay me any heed."

"And if he should send his messenger to you this afternoon?" his sister asked, gently. "If he should dare to beg you to come and take him from Lord Grigson's townhouse – or wherever they end up – then what shall you do? After all, it has been your practice to do just as our brother demands and to go to collect him from whatever difficulty he has tied himself into."

"I have already stated clearly that I will not do so again." The worry in his stomach twisted from side to side as he spoke but his resolve remained steady. "I am aware that it may bring him further difficulty but I cannot continue to do as he demands. I was glad that your husband thought to say it."

"As was I," Julia replied, smiling at him. "You have such a kind and generous heart, Denfield, I did not think that you would even *see* the advantage he was taking of you."

Peter let out a heavy breath, his tension beginning to fade. "Even if I did, I certainly would not have stepped back from it without Lord Symington's encouragements. Whatever are we to do, Julia?" Coming to a stop, he released his sister's arm and turned around to see Miss Jennings again. She was laughing still, a bright smile on her face, her green eyes sparkling in the summer sunshine as her dark curls danced lightly in the warm breeze. "I do not like to leave this matter unresolved."

"You may have to. The only thing you could think to do would be to apologise for our brother's *lack* of apology. But we cannot force Henley to do as he must."

Shame climbed quickly up Peter's spine and he closed his eyes. "I do not want to have to do such a thing."

"Then do not," came the quiet reply. "But Miss Jennings will be left wondering and waiting for many a week for Henley to apologise otherwise. I suppose, Denfield, that it is entirely up to you."

"The trouble is, I cannot get her from my thoughts," Peter confessed, seeing his sister's eyes round in obvious surprise. "I do not mean that I find her so desirous that I cannot stop thinking about her or any such thing as that. It is only that her injury seemed so very bad and the way that she could not walk without aid for some days and still cannot dance... the very minimum she requires from us is an apology!"

"Not from us but from Henley," his sister reminded him, looping her arm back through his again and pulling him away from gazing at Miss Jennings. "I do wonder if there is more to your consideration of her than you might have considered, however."

A frown tugged at Peter's eyebrows. "What do you mean?"

"I mean that you might well be considering her in perhaps a more... affectionate light than you first thought."

Rather astonished, Peter shot her a sharp look only to see her smile, her eyes alight with questions, though he quickly shook his head. "Certainly not. As I told your husband recently, I have no interest whatsoever in finding a match of my own and certainly would never permit my heart to have any affection for whoever I end up taking as my bride."

"No?" Julia tilted her head a little, searching his face as though she hoped to find a different answer. "What is it, then, that you would look for?"

"It must be nothing but practicality," Peter replied, aware of how his heart began to ache in sudden protest as though it agreed with all that Julia was saying. "When I take a bride, she must satisfy all my requirements and able to be all I desire."

Julia wrinkled her nose. "And by that, you mean that you expect her to play the pianoforte brilliantly, to be able to paint and draw with great skill, to sing like a bird, to dance without ever making a mistake, to hold a conversation with just the *right* amount of engagement, to always be respectful, genteel and amiable no matter the circumstances. Is that not right?"

Considering this, Peter shrugged lightly. "I should like her also to be able to ride."

"Denfield!" The astonishment in Julia's voice had him stopping, turning to look at her again rather than walking together. "You are not being truthful at this moment, are you?"

A little confused, he paused before answering. "Why, yes. I am."

"You would have all these expectations and requirements for whichever young lady you might consider?"

"I would."

"And if she should fail in one or more aspects?"

The answer seemed clear enough to Peter and he spread his hands wide. "Then I would not consider her any longer."

"But that is ridiculous! You will never find *any* young lady who can be all those things together! She will, no doubt, fail in some endeavour and certainly can never always be cheerful and amiable as you expect. What if she is sorrowful over something? What if she is tired? Will you expect her then to pin a smile to her face for you and pretend all is well?"

"I... " Peter trailed off, his brows knotting. "I do not know. I did not think about such a scenario."

"And what if *you* do not meet the requirements for the young lady that you end up pursuing?" his sister challenged, eyebrows lifting. "What then?"

Peter's lips quirked, his frown fading. "My dear sister, I do not think that any young lady would be able to find fault in what I could offer."

"Ah, but you do not hunt," his sister challenged, her hands going to her hips. "What if she decides that, for *her*, she must have a gentleman who can hunt. She must also, in fact, have a gentleman who will dance every dance with her and who will not grumble about taking her to the dance floor."

Peter scowled. "You know very well that a gentleman is not expected always to dance."

"Ah, but it *is* expected by some ladies, if not by most," came the swift reply, "just as some gentlemen might expect a lady to have a proficiency in riding. You cannot complain about that, surely."

With a roll of his eyes whilst trying to ignore the way his sister's words were beginning to burn through him and ignite his conscience, Peter turned back to begin walking again. "You are being foolish, Julia."

"I am not the one displaying any sort of foolishness," she challenged, quickly though falling into step with him at the same time. "You have high standards, brother and you may find that, should you let yourself free of them, something more important would take its place."

"Something more important?" Peter challenged, as his sister nodded. "You speak of affection."

48

The smile which spread across her face and the light which shone in her eyes could not permit his frustration to grow any bigger and, with a sigh, he shook his head.

"Your husband already spoke of such a thing to me, my dear but I do not think that I am inclined towards such a thing. I would rather be considered practical."

"Could you not be both?" Julia settled her hand on his arm again, their argument already fading into harmony. "Could you not be considered, practical and open to affection, should it come?"

For a few moments, Peter considered this but did not speak. His heart leapt as Miss Jennings came to mind but he quickly threw the image of her away. Seeing Julia looking at him for a response and not wanting to hurt her, he said the only thing he could think of. "I shall consider it, Julia." Seeing her smile, he lifted his shoulders and let them fall. "There can be no harm in that, I am sure."

Chapter Seven

"Are you quite sure you will be able to dance?"

Anne nodded even though her own worries were already beginning to spiral within her like a strong wind. "Yes, Aunt. My ankle has not pained me in some days."

"Which I am glad for but for which I do not want you to overdo it and then cause yourself more pain."

Seeing the concern in Lady Mayhew's eyes, Anne offered her a small smile as they stepped into the ballroom together. "I am sure that there is nothing to be worried about, Aunt. I did practise with the dancing master this afternoon and all went very well."

"Yes, but that is not the same as dancing with gentlemen who might very well be inclined to stamp on your feet inadvertently, depending on their grace and on how much they have imbibed!"

"That is true, I suppose, though mayhap no-one shall want to dance with me and all will be well."

The hitched breath from Lady Mayhew let Anne know that such a thought was, perhaps, even worse than the concern over her ankle, though she did not say anything more but only smiled instead.

"You will be certain to have your dance card filled this evening, should you wish it to be," Lady Mayhew replied, steadily. "After the incident with Lord Henley, it seems as though everyone in the *ton* wishes to know who you are and what has taken place. Though," she considered, giving Anne a quick, wry smile, "I am not convinced that speaking with gossip mongers is an acceptable idea."

"Certainly, I would agree," Anne laughed, despite her own uncertainty still delving deep within her. "Perhaps Lady Grace shall be present this evening also. I should very much like to see her again."

Lady Mayhew smiled. "It is good to see that you have made such a dear friend in Lady Grace this last week. I think her quite a remarkable and very genteel young lady, though she does have that determination within her which some might consider... a little disagreeable."

"I do not. In fact, I believe that I envy her a little."

Looking at her in surprise, Lady Mayhew lifted an eyebrow. "You envy her confidence?"

"Yes I do, just as I envied my sisters," Anne replied, truthfully. "There is an ease of manner that I lack and I do not much like it. I hate how I trip over words, how the simplest of questions from a gentleman makes my tongue stick to the roof of my mouth as I struggle to find a suitable response. I despise how my hands go clammy, how my stomach writhes and twists. How much easier it would be to have the confidence that Lady Grace possesses!"

"You can have that very same confidence but it will take time and it will take effort on your part," Lady Mayhew replied, gently. "Already, you are a good deal better than you were before. When you first came to London, you could not even look a gentleman in the eye without going red in the face and now you are able to hold a small conversation. You have had both gentlemen and ladies surrounding you and you have done remarkably well for someone so shy."

Anne allowed the compliments to settle on her heart rather than pushing them away, taking in a deep breath and then releasing it slowly as she lifted her chin just a little, sensing the heaviness going from her just a little. "I suppose that is true." Her happiness began to break apart as she remembered the bet Lady Mayhew had made with her father. "Though I do not know if I shall improve enough for a gentleman to consider me *this* Season... and if I do not, if I fail, then my father will – "

"You will not fail," Lady Mayhew interrupted, crisply. "You will succeed. I have every confidence in you and you ought to have a little more faith in yourself!"

"Lady Mayhew, Miss Jennings, good evening."

Anne smiled quickly as a gentleman already known to her – Lord Grigson – bowed in front of them both. He was a handsome fellow though known to be something of a rogue when he chose to be. Her aunt had already told her she might dance with him and the like was not to do anything other than that. If he asked to call on her or to walk in the park with him, then she would have to find a way to graciously refuse.

"Good evening," she replied, seeing him smiling broadly at

her. "You are enjoying the ball thus far, I hope?" Relieved that she had managed to ask a question without a tremble in her voice or a stutter over some of her words, Anne kept her smile fixed as Lord Grigson nodded fervently.

"I have, though I should ask you if I might sign your dance card, Miss Jennings and thereafter, take a turn with you about the room?"

"It would be my pleasure."

Anne closed her eyes in embarrassment the very moment she answered, though she had little choice but to take her dance card from her wrist and hand it to him. She had meant only to accept the offer of a dance from Lord Grigson but instead had managed to accept both the dance and the turn about the room. She shot an apologetic glance to her aunt but Lady Mayhew only smiled and shrugged lightly. If Anne took a turn about the room with him, Anne had very little doubt that her aunt would stay close by.

"Excellent, I have chosen the polka. A very fine dance indeed, I think!" With a flourish, Lord Grigson handed the dance card back to Anne and then turned to stand beside her, offering her his arm. "Shall we?"

"Of course." She could not find the words to refuse, could not find any excuse to give him and thus, placing her hand on his arm and trusting that her aunt would follow, Anne walked side by side with Lord Grigson as he led her about the room.

"It is a very fine ball, is it not?" he asked, his tone jovial. "I had thought it rather crowded when I first arrived but since the drawing room, parlour and card room are open to us all, it now feels a little less constrictive."

"Yes, I would agree." Anne did not know what else to say, finding herself questioning whether she should ask him something else or wait for him to speak. Even if she *did* have a question to ask him, which one would it be? What would she choose? Worried that she would make some sort of mistake, Anne swallowed hard and chose to remain silent. They walked this way for some minutes, only for Anne to realize that Lord Grigson was leading her to the corner of the room. That, she considered, was a little disconcerting for there were too many shadows there and, mayhap, gentlemen within those shadows that she did not want to be seen with.

Glancing over her shoulder, she tried to see her aunt but Lady Mayhew was nowhere to be seen.

"I think I should return to my aunt now," she quavered, hearing the wobble in her voice though Lord Grigson only laughed.

"There is no need for any rush. Only a few more minutes, Miss Jennings. I have someone here who wishes to speak with you."

"Speak with me?" Anne repeated, though Lord Grigson said nothing further, continuing to amble with her alongside him. Anne made to pull her hand from his arm and turn away but Lord Grigson was too quick for her. Perhaps sensing that she had been about to do that very thing, he set his hand atop hers, pinning it there and keeping her with him.

Fear clawed in Anne's throat.

"It is only Lord Henley," Lord Grigson told her, mayhap sensing her fright. "He does not want to be seen apologising for he is a little too mean-spirited to make himself so humble. I am sure you understand."

Anne could say nothing, her eyes rounding as she took in the sight of Lord Henley who was lounging in one of the chairs near to the wall, his legs outstretched and crossed at the ankle as a lazy smile ran along his face at the sight of her.

"Ah, Miss Jennings!" he exclaimed, his words coming out so slowly it was as if he were too lazy to speak with any great strength. "I see that Lord Grigson has managed to spirit you here. I do hope you will forgive him for that. It was at my request and he truly is a good friend."

Anne was finally permitted to let her hands loose though when she took a step back, Lord Grigson was already there, keeping her in between the chairs and himself. *Where is my aunt?*

"You are owed an apology, it seems." Lord Henley pushed himself out of his chair with a great and heavy sigh, though his smile still lingered on his face which, for whatever reason, unsettled Anne a great deal. Her skin crawled as he reached out one hand to take hers, her arm stiff as he lifted it.

"You were injured by my foolishness," Lord Henley continued, though his words began to slip into one another, making Anne realize that he had already drank a great deal of the whisky and the brandy which was present. "I fell on you, did I not?"

He laughed as Lord Grigson himself snorted with laughter, though Anne's face flushed with both embarrassment and upset. Had she not been between two chairs – one on either side and had not Lord Grigson been behind her, then she would have quit their company already but, as such, she could not.

"I hear you could not dance for some days, which must have been a great trial for someone as pretty as you."

A fresh wave of fear crested over Anne as she looked back into Lord Henley's face and saw his eyes suddenly watchful. "There is no need to apologise, " she said, hoarsely. "Do excuse me. I must return to my aunt."

"Oh, but I should like to make my apologies *more* than evident," Lord Henley replied, grinning as his fingers tightened around hers. "You are a charming young lady, I hear and I must admit, a good deal more pleasant than I remembered."

Anne stiffened, her chin lifting a fraction "I do not care what you think of my appearance. I wish to return to my aunt."

"All in good time, all in good time." Lord Henley threw a grin to his friend, who only chuckled. Anne glanced again over her shoulder but there was no sign of her aunt. Would she even see her in this gloom? Everything in her screamed for her to escape but there was nowhere for her to go, nowhere for her to hide. *I have to be strong.*

"Do excuse me, Lord Henley," she said as firmly as she dared. "I must take my leave now."

Again, his fingers tightened on her hand and, to her horror, he bent his head and pressed a kiss to her knuckles. This brought her no sensation of joy, no happiness or contentment but rather a deep and concerning fear. She tried to pull her hand away but Lord Henley was too strong, his grip tightening until it was painful.

"I think you *are* rather beautiful," he murmured, growing so close to her, she could feel his breath on her face. "Charming, beautiful and delightful. Tell me, Miss Jennings, are you considering marriage or looking for something – or someone – a little more at ease with such things?"

A cold hand gripped her heart and she tried to pull away from him again. "What I am is a lady with a sterling reputation and one I do not need to be tainted in any way."

Lord Henley laughed, coming so close that she could see the

flecks of green in his eyes. "Ah, but perhaps I might be able to convince you otherwise."

His arms snaked about her waist and his head leaned down, attempting to kiss her and Anne let out a cry of fright. Making to pull back, she staggered backwards before losing her footing and falling backwards – and taking Lord Henley with her.

Chapter Eight

"What is he *doing*?"

Peter stared aghast as his brother took Miss Jennings' hand and pressed his mouth to it. The lady was clearly uncomfortable as she pulled her hand away but from where he stood, it appeared that Henley would not release it.

"Where is Lady Mayhew, Miss Jennings' aunt?" Lord Symington asked, looking all around. "She is usually so very vigilant. I am surprised that she is not with Miss Jennings at this moment."

"We must interrupt," Peter stated, disliking his brother's smile and how he drew so close to Miss Jennings. "Come, Symington, Julia. If Lady Mayhew has been delayed for some reason, then Miss Jennings' ought to have another lady with her just to ensure that her reputation - !"

His words came to a dead stop as he saw his brother lean forward, his arms going about Miss Jennings' waist as he attempted to kiss her. His whole body froze, his blood freezing in his veins as the sheer horror of what his brother was doing hit him right between the eyes. And then he was moving forward, hurrying towards them, seeing how Miss Jennings staggered back, seeing her foot slipping, the heavy weight of Lord Henley pushing her backwards… and with his arms outstretched, Peter managed to catch her before she fell to the floor, though his brother fell with her and, somehow, managed to roll to one side and collapse completely to the floor. There came a howl of pain, a gush of blood as Henley clutched at his nose, leaving Peter to stare down into the white face of Miss Jennings.

"Are you quite all right, Miss Jennings?" Peter tried to release her but her hands were digging into his coat lapels, clinging to him for dear life. "I cannot tell you – "

"Whatever is going on here?"

Peter turned his head to see a lady approaching, her eyes narrowed in his direction and her hands going to her waist, elbows akimbo. She eyed them suspiciously, much to his horror, Peter watched a few others begin to draw closer to them, having been drawn either by his brother's loud exclamation or this lady's question.

"Miss Jennings," he murmured, looking down at her. "I – I am sorry." An idea came into his mind and he instantly pushed it away, having no desire to do what was being presented to him but slowly realizing that he had very little choice *but* to do this. It was not fair to Miss Jennings that his brother had chosen to act in such a way. It would not be right if her reputation was ruined, if it was blackened and darkened because of Henley's behavior. She would have no future. No-one would want to marry her, no-one would ever consider her! He had no choice. He only hoped she would accept him.

"Explain yourself!" the lady cried, making Peter draw in a deep breath and, turning towards the woman, smiled as broadly as he could.

"You will have to forgive me," he said, disentangling himself from Miss Jennings as best he could, though he made sure to put her arm though his so she might have his support. "I have, only just now, asked Miss Jennings to marry me... and my brother was so surprised at my action, he fell and has injured himself quite severely, I think."

A murmur of voices ran around the group watching and Peter instantly heard Miss Jennings' swift intake of breath, glancing at her and seeing her wide eyes and pale face.

"I hope you understand," he whispered to her, seeing her blink rapidly. "We must marry. I will not have you ruined because of my brother's foolishness."

"Denfield!" Julia exclaimed, though her voice was nothing louder than a whisper. "What is happening? What are you doing?"

"Are you certain about this?" Miss Jennings whispered, her voice cracking as he nodded. "You might have anyone you wish and – "

"Are you informing me that you are now engaged, Lord Denfield?" The lady who had spied them at the first came closer, her eyes sharp, her distrust evident. "You are engaged to Miss Jennings?"

Behind her, a crowd began to form and Peter's stomach twisted, looking to Miss Jennings, seeing her eyes now flooded with tears though she did not let a single one fall. He waited for her to look at him, caught the almost indiscernible nod and, with

57

another breath, turned back to the crowd. "You have heard correctly," he said, as loud as he dared. "Miss Jennings and I are to be wed!"

What followed was such a loud exclamation and such a hubbub of voices, Peter did not know what to do or where to look. Behind him, two footmen were helping Lord Henley from the floor, his shirt stained with blood and one hand clutching at his nose. Beside him, Julia and Lord Symington were staring at him with such shock evident on their faces, he feared that the *ton* would take note of it and realize that this whole thing had happened only in the last few moments.

"Anne?" A lady Peter recognized as Lady Mayhew came hurrying forward, her hands outstretched to catch Miss Jennings' in her own. "You must forgive me, I was caught by an old friend who simply would not let me leave after you and who persuaded me that you would be quite all right with Lord Grigson... though you are not with him now, I see." Her eyebrows furrowed, looking to Peter and he offered her a tiny smile in return.

"Please do not exclaim, Lady Mayhew, but I have just declared Miss Jennings and I engaged."

Lady Mayhew did not let out any sort of exclamation, did not even squeak in surprise but rather, simply stared at him as the remaining color drained from her face.

"We will talk about this all later, Aunt, but for the moment, you must smile and acknowledge our engagement with as much enthusiasm as you can muster." Miss Jennings spoke clearly but with still such a wobble in her voice, Peter's heart tore for her. How much she had endured at the hands of his brother? And what would she think of *him* in doing what he had done? Would she think him just as poorly behaved as Henley?

"Good gracious." Lady Mayhew took in a long breath and then closed her eyes, before forcing a smile that did not spread to her eyes. "You are all right however, Anne?"

"I am." Miss Jennings reached out and squeezed her aunt's arm. "But I am now engaged to be married and must appear as joyous as can be. Lord Denfield, might you call tomorrow?"

Peter nodded quickly, a little relieved at how well Miss Jennings was taking this, how clear she seemed to be in understanding what had to be done. "Of course. At your earliest

58

convenience."

Lady Mayhew looked at him dead in the eye, her expression firm. "You fully intend to marry my niece? You do not intend to break things off before the wedding?"

Peter put one hand to his heart, understanding her concern and where it came from. "I give you my word."

"Then I promise you that I shall smile and be as happy as you wish me to be," Lady Mayhew replied, turning back to face the crowd who were still excitedly talking to each other while glancing often in Peter and Miss Jennings' direction. "Until tomorrow, Lord Denfield."

"Thank you, Lady Mayhew," Peter answered, softly. "Until tomorrow."

***

"You are engaged, then?"

Julia flopped into a chair, with her husband quickly handing her a small measure of brandy in a patterned glass. "You are truly going to marry Miss Jennings?"

"I am." Peter took the glass from his brother-in-law, offering him a grim smile as he lifted it in a half-toast. "I could not permit Miss Jennings to be so disgraced."

"You could have forced your brother to marry her," Lord Symington suggested, sitting down as Peter shook his head. "It might have forced him to behave in a more appropriate manner."

"I could not do such a thing to the lady. She has already endured enough," Peter replied, seeing his sister nod. "If Miss Jennings was to be forced to marry my brother, then what life would that be? I could give her no assurance that Lord Henley would do as he ought to do, could not promise that she would have a life of enjoyment or happiness. Indeed, all I could promise her would have been that Henley would have been a neglectful and inconsiderate husband."

Silence filled the room for a few moments as they all considered the truth of Peter's statement. Peter himself let out a slow breath, his eyes closing as he considered the enormity of what had taken place. He was no longer to be a gentleman alone. Instead, in a few short months, he would be married and married

59

to a lady of whom he knew very little. Miss Jennings was almost a stranger to him, given that they were not well acquainted and yet she was the one whom he would take as a wife.

"Suppose she does not meet all of your requirements." Julia's lips quirked just a little as Peter shot her a dark look. "What will you do then?"

"I do not care about such things," Peter replied, truthfully. "My only thought as I stood with Miss Jennings in my arms, was how I was to go about protecting her, how I was to make certain that she did not face a life of sorrow given that nothing of what took place was her fault."

"It is most admirable," Lord Symington murmured, shaking his head to himself, "and not something that every gentleman would have done."

Peter shrugged but remained silent. It was not as though he had any intention of accepting praise in this matter. He had done what was right and that was all. He did not need to be applauded for it. Time and again, his thoughts returned to Miss Jennings, recalling how white her face had been, how tears had filled her eyes as she had realized the circumstances in which she now found herself.

"It is not I who requires praise," he said slowly, half to himself, "but rather, Miss Jennings. She has accepted injury, has accepted the lack of apology from our brother and has now accepted my hand without so much as a word of complaint. She might have wished to choose her own husband, might have wanted to be courted, to be walked with, danced with and sent all manner of gifts from her beau before being offered their hand in marriage. Now all of that is taken from her." His heart ached heavily and he closed his eyes, his face heating. "I do despise what our brother has done."

Julia took a sip of her brandy and let out a breath, her eyes a little red as though she had been attempting to hold back the tears for some time. "He was so close to bringing disgrace upon us all."

"Though he has broken his nose at least," Lord Symington shrugged, making Peter smile ruefully. "That will prevent him from any sort of foolishness for a time, I am sure. He will need to rest and recover and certainly cannot go about as he has been doing for fear that he will do himself further injury – especially since you are not to go pursuing after him, Denfield."

Peter's jaw tightened, a streak of anger running straight down his spine. "I shall never go to his aid again," he stated, fury rising in him. "After what he did this evening, I think him entirely unworthy of both our respect and our friendship. We may be kin, we may be family but I will not permit myself to be involved in *any* matter of his, no matter how small or how great." With a nod to himself, he looked first to Julia and then to Lord Symington. "My only consideration, my first priority, is to Miss Jennings and it is to *her* that I commit myself. From this day on, I shall be at *her* call rather than to Henley's. She can be assured of that."

Chapter Nine

"Are you able to tell me now what took place?"

Anne nodded, reaching for her tea cup. Her aunt had not pressed her the previous evening and she was grateful for it, given how weak and tired she had felt herself become. "I can."

"Only if you are ready," her aunt said, her worry evident in the way she gazed into Anne's face. "If you are not, then I am more than able – more than willing – to wait for you."

Anne shook her head. "It is better if I speak of it, I think. In truth, I am still a little overcome with all that took place and the situation I now find myself in."

Lady Mayhew nodded but did not say anything more, leaving her space to speak whenever she was ready. With a small breath, Anne closed her eyes and then began.

"You recall that Lord Grigson asked to take a turn with me about the room?" Opening her eyes, she saw her aunt nodding. "Lord Grigson was amiable at first but when I turned around to look for you and saw that you were not behind me, I begged him to wait."

With a slight frown, Lady Mayhew spread out her hands. "I am sorry that I did not manage to keep pace with you both. I was caught by an old – and very dear – friend and when I spoke with her and said that I was watching you, that I was attempting to accompany you alongside Lord Grigson, she told me not to worry and that Lord Grigson was a respectable sort and would bring you back very soon."

"Mayhap he would have done," Anne answered, not wanting her aunt to feel any sort of guilt over what had happened. "Had he not had this other errand from Lord Henley, then I might very well have been returned to you without incident. However, when I tried to depart from Lord Grigson's company, he would not permit me to leave him and, unfortunately, told me that I would have to go with him."

"To where Lord Henley sat."

Anne nodded, a slight shudder rushing through her frame as she recalled the shadows seeping around Lord Henley. To her mind, it had felt as though she had been walking into a dark and dreadful circumstance, as though the shadows themselves were a warning, a foreboding of what was to come and she had been entirely powerless to escape.

"When Lord Grigson finally released my hand, I thought to move away from him but instead, he stood behind me so I could not make my escape," she explained, aware of the slight tremble in her voice. "There were some chairs either side of me and Lord Henley in front of me so I had no other choice but to stand near him."

Lady Mayhew closed her eyes tightly. "Oh, my dear."

"I did not know what it was he wanted or what he intended," Anne continued, "though I do not think that he wanted to... do what he did in the end. I have no thought that such an action was something he had considered and planned."

"What do you mean?"

Trying to find the words to explain herself, Anne paused for a moment and then spread out her hands. "He told me that from what he understood, I was owed an apology from him. He grasped my hand and when he stood, it was then that I realised he had already imbibed a great deal."

A heavy sigh came from Lady Mayhew though her eyes opened this time. "I am sorry. I would have thought that the gentleman would have learned from the last time he had an encounter with you – again, when he had imbibed far too much!"

"I do not think that he did," Anne replied, with a slightly wry smile though that quickly fell away. "Lord Henley lifted my hand and, to my great dislike, pressed a kiss to my knuckles. When he looked at me again, however, there was something in his eyes which worried me a great deal. Then he... he... " Her eyes closed as she fought the panic which suddenly wrapped around her heart. "Then he made to try to kiss me, I believe. I stepped back in fright and, given that his hand was still tight around mine, he fell forward with me. I thought I was going to fall to the floor and hit my head but Lord Denfield appeared from somewhere – I do not know where – and caught me before I could do so. His brother fell to the ground, however, and, I believe hurt his nose. I heard someone say that it had broken!"

"Which is no less than he deserves, given what he tried to do!" Lady Mayhew exclaimed, sounding furious. "I am surprised that Lord Denfield did not step in *before* his brother attempted to do such a thing."

"I do not think he knew that Lord Henley would attempt to kiss me," Anne answered, quickly. "The shock on his face, the horror in his expression told me a good deal more than any words might have expressed."

This seemed to satisfy Lady Mayhew a little more for she nodded slowly and then reached to pick up her tea though Anne frowned at the way her hand trembled just a little as she set the tea cup back on the saucer.

"I am quite all right, however, Aunt," she said, in the hope of reassuring Lady Mayhew. "I was not in any way injured."

"Though Lady Newmarket and many others then spied you with Lord Denfield's arms about your waist."

Anne nodded, her eyes darting to her own tea cup rather than look at her aunt. Lord Henley trying to kiss her had come as a great shock, certainly, but to then find herself engaged was quite another. "Lord Denfield was only doing what he could to make certain I was protected from his brother and that I was not about to collapse from either injury or into a faint," she said, softly. "Lady Newmarket – or whoever it was – demanded to know what was taking place and Lord Denfield, after murmuring an apology to me, stated that he had just asked me to marry him and that I had accepted."

Lady Mayhew frowned. "He apologised?"

"I think it was to express sorrow over what his brother had done *and* to say that he was not about to do what he did without good reason, clearly aware that I was to have no say in the matter."

"I see." The frown lifted from Lady Mayhew's face. "And then that was all?"

Anne considered, trying to remember. "When there was a great hubbub of conversation and the like, after he had made that particular announcement, he did speak to me again – quietly, of course – to say how he hoped I understood and also to say that he would not see me ruined because of his brother's foolishness."

Lady Mayhew's shoulders dropped just a little. "I see. That was very good of him."

"I think he is a respectable fellow," Anne replied, her gaze now at the window rather than her aunt. "I do not know many gentlemen who would do such a thing as that."

"Yes, I would agree. Though I do wish the entire situation had not happened. Whatever was Lord Henley thinking?"

"I do not believe he did any thinking whatsoever." Anne swallowed hard, tears burning behind her eyes. "But now I am engaged to a gentleman who is practically a stranger to me! I do not know his character at all, I do not know a thing about him save for the fact that he has a brother who cannot behave as a gentleman ought."

"That is not true," her aunt countered quickly, perhaps hearing the desperation growing in Anne's voice. "We know that he is an honourable gentleman at least and that should count for a great deal. After all, when you were first injured by his brother, did he not come to apologise on his brother's behalf? And then, did he not speak to you regretfully about Lord Henley's lack of willingness to apologise to you in person?"

Anne nodded, blinking back her tears. "Yes, he did."

"And, as you yourself said, he did not want to see you disgraced by his brother's behaviour and thus, made certain that your reputation would be protected by offering you his hand. He did not have to do such a thing. There was an alternative."

A little confused, Anne looked back at her aunt. "What alternative?"

"Well, he might easily have said that his *brother* had asked you to marry him and that you had accepted." Lady Mayhew offered her a small, slightly sad smile. "Did you not think of that?"

Anne's heart catapulted around in her chest, her whole body suddenly tingling with what she recognized as sheer horror of what she might have been faced with, had not Lord Denfield offered to marry her. "Perhaps he knew that his brother would refuse to marry me."

"That may be true but I think there is more to it than that," came the reply. "My dear niece, I think Lord Denfield is an honourable gentleman and one with a good heart because he could not bring himself to see *you* wed to his brother – even though he had every right to insist that such a match took place. If he saw Lord Henley attempt to kiss you, then he would have been able to stand in front of society and tell them all he had witnessed so that a marriage would take place. He did not, however. Instead, he gave up his own freedom, his own right to choose a bride for himself and took you in that place without even a moment to think." She smiled gently. "From what you have said, it does not sound as though he hesitated."

"He... he did not." Anne's voice had grown quieter. "Now that I think of it, he did not even give the situation a moment of consideration. He knew what he had to do and he did it."

"Precisely," her aunt replied. "So though you do not know Lord Denfield well, I can assure you that he is an honourable gentleman. He will not reject you. He will not turn away from you. If you recall, I asked him last evening if he intended to marry you, that he truly would do such a thing rather than pretend for a few days before ending the engagement and he gave me such a solemn look and such a promise that I believed him without question."

A gentle relief stole away some of the tension from Anne's frame. "That is good, I think."

"Yes, it is." Lady Mayhew leaned forward to pick up her tea cup again. "You have been saved from a great deal by the hand of Lord Denfield. That is a relief, though he must be so very ashamed of his brother."

Anne hesitated, thinking of what had taken place and recalling how Lord Denfield had thrown rather a disgusted look to his brother as he had writhed about on the floor. "It must be very trying for him, attempting to keep his brother from acting in that way, given that Lord Henley seems entirely unwilling to listen to him."

Her aunt scowled. "Some gentlemen do not know what it is to behave well," she said, her tone a little caustic. "And as for Lord Grigson, I fully intend to speak to *him* whenever I should see him next!"

"I do not think he knew what Lord Henley was going to do. I did not see him thereafter and I believe he must have hurried away for fear of being caught by the gossip-mongers."

"Then he is a coward," Lady Mayhew declared, firmly. "And I have every intention of telling him so."

Anne opened her mouth to say that mayhap, Lord Grigson would run from Lady Mayhew when she attempted to speak so, only for there to come a rap at the door. Lady Mayhew called for the servant to enter and he did so at once, holding a letter out to Lady Mayhew first of all, and then two to Anne herself. Anne took them with a murmur of thanks as Lady Mayhew dismissed the servant.

"This is from your father, I think." Turning the letter over, she broke the seal and then unfolded it. "I shall be very glad indeed to write to him to inform him of your engagement. Although... " Trailing off, she lifted her gaze back to Anne. "You are over the age required for your father's consent."

Anne said nothing, seeing her aunt's thoughts flying through her eyes like shooting stars.

"I do not think I shall inform him of your engagement," Lady Mayhew said briskly, throwing the letter down on the table in clear disgust. "He writes to say that he is sure I will have failed and that his door is open for our return at any moment and I fear that, should I write to him about your engagement, he might attempt to make certain that the marriage does not go ahead."

Anne's stomach twisted. "Why should he do that?"

"Because having a spinster daughter does bring some relief with it," Lady Mayhew replied with a small, sad smile. "It means that he can leave you with the running of the house and the like, expect you to do all that he asks of you without complaint and can threaten you with a lack of security if you do not."

A shudder ran through Anne's frame.

"Therefore, I will not inform him of your engagement at all, just to be certain that he will not do anything to try and impede it," her aunt finished, firmly. "You can write to him yourself, if you wish, when you are Lady Denfield, and see what kind of response you gain from him!" A warm, encouraging smile spread across her face and Anne managed to return it, though she did not feel the same hope as was clearly displayed in her aunt's words. "Who has written to you?"

"I have two letters," Anne replied, picking up the first and recognizing the seal at once. "This is from Lady Grace, no doubt asking me what has taken place and demanding to know when she can come to call." She gave her aunt a smile before picking up her second letter. "And this... this one I do not know." Frowning, she broke the seal, not recognizing the crest pressed into the wax and then opened it out. The few short lines made her heart jump, nervousness running through her veins as she pressed her lips tight together, telling herself quietly that all would be well.

"The second, my dear?"

"Is from Lord Denfield." Lifting her gaze, she tried to smile at her aunt again but her lips refused to move. "He wishes to come to call, just as you asked him."

"Very good. When?"

"This afternoon," Anne replied, looking back at the letter again. "He wishes to bring his sister also so that we might discuss our wedding plans." Her aunt said something but Anne did not hear it, her mind whirring with a sudden realization that soon, she would be married to Lord Denfield, soon she would find herself as mistress to Denfield estate and be expected to be to him all that a wife ought.

But I do not know him! her heart cried, fear beginning to force its way back through her again. *And what if, despite his honourable actions, he turns out to be even worse than his brother?*

Chapter Ten

Peter cleared his throat, lifted his chin and rapped smartly on the large wooden door. It was opened to him and to Julia at once and he was welcomed inside by a butler who clearly knew who he was and that he had been expected.

"Lord Denfield, please do come in."

"Thank you."

"Lady Symington," the butler murmured, taking all of their things from them. "Might I then bring you this way? Lady Mayhew and Miss Jennings are waiting for you in the drawing room."

Peter offered his arm to his sister and together, they walked down the hallway towards the drawing room. When he had informed his sister and Lord Symington that he was going to be meeting with Miss Jennings, Julia had asked to accompany him, stating that it was important for Miss Jennings to know Peter's family – and to be sure that they were not all as dreadful as Henley! Peter had accepted quickly, feeling it almost a relief that Julia would be with him and that he would not be alone. His desire, at this juncture, was to make certain that Miss Jennings felt as at ease about this situation as she could and getting to know Julia might very well help with that.

"Lord Denfield and Lady Symington," the butler announced as Peter walked into the room. Miss Jennings and Lady Mayhew were already standing and though Miss Jennings bobbed a curtsy, Lady Mayhew only stood tall and surveyed first Peter and then Julia, though Peter did not blame her for that. This was a very strange and unexpected situation and after how his brother had treated Lady Mayhew's niece, Peter could not be surprised at her wariness.

"Please, do come and sit down." Lady Mayhew's voice was thin though she did smile briefly. Peter came a little further into the room but before he could sit, introduced his sister to them both.

"I thought, Miss Jennings, it might be appropriate to bring my sister with me," he said, quietly. "Might I present Lady Julia Symington? Julia, this is Miss Jennings and her aunt, Lady Mayhew."

Julia smiled warmly at the two ladies. "I am delighted to make your acquaintance, truly. Though," she continued, her smile slipping just a little, "I am sorry for the circumstances."

"As am I," Peter said quickly, seeing Miss Jennings look away, her face hidden from him for a moment as she made to sit down. "It is the second occasion that my brother has behaved poorly and I am truly horrified at his actions."

"I could not quite believe what I was seeing!" Julia exclaimed, shaking her head as she sat down too. "My brother is known to be rather foolish in certain aspects of his life, Miss Jennings, but I never imagined that he would do something as dreadful as that."

There came a moment of silence and Peter found himself suddenly not sure of where to look or of what to say. Miss Jennings was studying her hands as they were clasped in her lap, Lady Mayhew was looking from him to Julia and back again and Julia was sitting with a soft smile on her lips though her eyes, when they looked at him, were worried.

"If you do not wish to commit to this engagement, Miss Jennings, there is no need for you to do so." Peter saw how her head lifted sharply, how her gaze went to his and heard Lady Mayhew's swift intake of breath. He had not meant to say such a thing but he had spoken it regardless. "I meant what I said, Miss Jennings. *I* am more than willing to marry you. I do not want you to bear any disgrace from the happenings with my brother. I am an honest gentleman, with a decent fortune and large estate. I would treat you with kindness all of my days and never be cruel. However, I am well aware that you do not know me and only have my word for such statements. If you do not desire to marry, if you wish to make your own choice, then in a fortnight or so, I will declare that *I* have ended the engagement so that the fault will fall solely upon my shoulders. You would be free again."

Miss Jennings closed her eyes and shook her head. "I do not think that such a thing would ever work successfully," she said, her voice quiet as she opened her eyes again to look at him. "Even if you were to end the engagement and take the blame for it being broken apart, the *ton* would still regard me in a different light. I would not be able to mend that."

"But in time," Peter interrupted quickly, spreading out his

70

hands. "Next Season, I am sure – "

"I do not have next Season." Miss Jennings' eyes settled on his, piercing in their fervency. "My father has stated that if I do not wed this Season, then I am to spend the rest of my days as a spinster, undertaking whatever duties my father chooses to assign me." Taking in a deep breath, she offered him the very smallest of smiles, one which did not send any light into her eyes. "As good as you are to ask me such a thing, I confess to you that I have no desire for this engagement to come to an end." Her eyes narrowed just a fraction. "If you are truly willing to continue to towards marriage, then I will accept you."

Peter let his hands clasp back together in his lap. "That is just as I have said, Miss Jennings. I am more than willing to continue towards matrimony."

"Excellent." As though she had been waiting for him to confirm such a thing, Lady Mayhew rose to her feet to ring the bell. "Shall we send for tea?"

"Yes, of course. Thank you, Aunt." Miss Jennings' smile was growing though, to Peter's mind, she still did not look particularly happy. There was no joy in her expression, no light in her eyes. This must still have been a great shock to her, he realized, and as yet, the thought of marrying him had still not quite settled in her mind.

"I did wonder, Miss Jennings, if – "

"Why do you not sit beside my niece, Lord Denfield?"

Peter looked to Lady Mayhew who was gesturing him over to her.

"I thank you. If it would be suitable then yes, I should be glad to."

"I should think that two betrothed people sitting beside one another would be more than appropriate," his sister replied, a tinkling laugh flowing from her. "Now, tell me, Lady Mayhew about your own circumstances, if you would. I should like to know you a little better, if I might."

With Lady Mayhew and his sister falling into conversation, that left Peter with Miss Jennings and, as he rose from his chair to come and sit with her, he saw the way that color instantly flooded through her cheeks.

"Might I sit with you, Miss Jennings?" Even though he had been given permission by her aunt, Peter wanted to make certain

71

that the lady herself was quiet content herself though, much to his relief, she nodded quickly. "I thank you." The moment he did so, however, a strange trembling seemed to push its way down Peter's arms and legs, going right to the very tips of his fingers. It was as if he were both nervous and delighted at the prospect of being so close to her, so near. Suddenly, his tongue stuck to the roof of his mouth and he could not think of what to say.

Silence grew between them and a glance to Miss Jennings told him that she was just as nervous as he was. The way her eyes danced from one place to the next, her lip catching between her teeth and the worried way she plucked at her gown gave the clear impression of her worry.

"We will have to spend some time together, Miss Jennings," Peter began, when she continued to remain silent. "We do not know one another at all, do we?"

"And yet we are engaged." She managed to smile at him though her eyes went somewhere towards his ear rather than looking into his face.

"Yes, we are." Again, Peter fought to find something to say to her, something that would help the conversation to flow. "Might you tell me about your family?"

"My family?" Her eyes flared when he nodded and then, within a moment, she was looking down at her clasped hands again, though Peter noticed just how white they were, given how tightly she gripped them together.

"Do you have any parents still living?"

Her eyes closed. "Yes." Her voice was quiet now, hoarse as though he were bringing up a great many emotions with his questions. "My father is at home."

"Oh." Peter frowned. "And he is not in London with you?" His answer was only a small shake of the head. "I am sorry for the loss of your mother."

Miss Jennings winced. "My mother has not passed away, Lord Denfield. It is only... " A heavy sigh came from her, her fingers still gripped tightly together. "Lord Denfield, I am not someone filled with confidence. I apologise for the struggle this conversation is causing you. Forgive me."

Peter's frown grew and he found himself leaning forward just a little, wanting to catch her attention though she still would not look at him. "Miss Jennings, I do not think this a struggle because of you. It is a stilted conversation because we are both thrust into the very same situation and are still – the both of us – coming to settle into it. If there is something that you do not wish to speak of, then that is quite all right. There is time enough for us to learn more from each other."

Miss Jennings swallowed hard and, finally, looked directly at him though, much to Peter's concern, her eyes were a little damp. Glancing to his sister and Lady Mayhew and seeing them both deeply involved in discussion, he boldly reached out and placed his hand on top of Miss Jennings' clenched ones. They were so very cold.

"There is no need to fear," he said, as softly as he could. "My brother is a dastardly rogue but I assure you, I am not anything like him. I will not harm you, insult you, berate you or force you to do or say anything you have no desire to do. If you do not wish to speak of your parents, then that presents no difficulty to me. I do hope you understand, Miss Jennings."

Her eyes were still looking into his, her lips trembling just a little though, after a moment, she closed them and let out a slow breath. "You will not be angry with my lack of confidence, Lord Denfield?" she asked, her voice a whisper. "My father always – "

"I should never dream of such a thing," Peter told her, firmly, a little frustrated that he had interrupted her but very much desiring her not to fear. "Timidity is not something to be ashamed of, Miss Jennings. It is something that must be faced, certainly, but you shall not be taken to task by me because of it." For a moment, he wondered what it was that Miss Jennings had been about to say about her father but, seeing the tea trays being brought in, he set the question aside and then lifted his hand from hers. That had been a short conversation but it had been a conversation nonetheless and Peter was grateful for it.

***

"Lord Denfield, might I speak with you for just a moment?"

Peter turned just to see Lady Mayhew hurrying from the drawing room towards him. They had only just taken their leave after sharing a tea tray and discussing a date for the upcoming wedding, which had now been set for seven weeks ahead. "Yes, of course, Lady Mayhew. Is everything quite all right?"

"Yes, it is only that there is a personal matter I wished to share with you."

"Do excuse me." Julia smiled and excused herself, leaving Peter and Lady Mayhew to stand alone together. Peter, watching her for a few moments, then turned back to Lady Mayhew with a small, expectant smile.

"It is about Anne – Miss Jennings," Lady Mayhew said, quickly. "And her father."

"Lord Ellon."

Lady Mayhew nodded. "He is married to my sister, you understand, Anne's mother. She is presently not at the estate nor in London but is residing with our *other* sister up in Scotland. However, I would beg of you *not* to write to Lord Ellon to ask for his permission to marry Anne."

Worry began to trace its way around Peter's heart. "I see."

"He is not required to give it, since Anne is of age," Lady Mayhew continued, her face a little flushed. "But I would also ask you because I fear that, should you do so, her father will do everything in his power to make certain that Anne remains as she is."

The worry tightened around Peter's heart. "Why would he do such a thing?"

"Because he is a brute," Lady Mayhew replied, sharply, her words stinging Peter even though they were not meant for him. "My sister – Anne's mother – has been threatened by him and now fears for her life! She has not returned to his side for some months and I have encouraged her to remain where she is in Scotland so that she might be safe." Lady Mayhew blinked as she came to a stop, perhaps having not meant to tell him so much.

"You can trust me in this, Lady Mayhew." Peter, seeing the fervency in Lady Mayhew's eyes and recalling how uncertain Miss Jennings had been when she had spoken, was inclined to believe every word. "Lord Ellon does not need to know of the engagement."

Relief had Lady Mayhew closing her eyes for a moment. "I thank you, Lord Denfield. As I have said, her father is a brute but he is also very aware of the fact that he might take his daughter and keep her a spinster in *his* service for as long as he lives. She will end up as nothing more than a drudge and all because he terrified her into this shy, uncertain creature that she is."

Sympathy began to billow in Peter's heart. "Your niece already apologised to me for her shy manner but I have encouraged her not to think of it as a dreadful thing or something that she is required to apologise to me for. I understand that our circumstances are rather unusual though I do hope to get to know Miss Jennings a good deal better over the next few weeks."

Lady Mayhew smiled and touched his arm for just a moment, her gratitude evident. "You will find my niece to be a caring, considerate young lady who is still learning about who she is and what she can achieve. Her two younger sisters are already wed and settled and had it not been for my presence at the last wedding, I believe that her father would have kept Anne back from society for good! Though I am a little disappointed in how things went as regards your brother's treatment of Anne, I will say that I am relieved to know that she will be married and she will be settled as mistress in her own right."

Peter smiled, finding himself almost happy at the thought of marrying Miss Jennings now. "I will do all that I can to encourage her to speak as she wishes and to be as free with me in conversation as she pleases," he promised. "I would like her to be happy, Lady Mayhew. After the brief things you have told me, I find myself all the more determined to offer that to her."

"You *are* a good sort," Lady Mayhew exclaimed, her lips curving into a warm smile. "I told her that you were."

Putting one hand to his heart, Peter bowed. "You are very kind to say so."

"I know that you are," Lady Mayhew replied, firmly. "After hearing what happened last evening, I realised that you could easily have insisted that your brother marry Anne but instead, you stepped in yourself."

A slight shadow passed over Peter's mind. "I would not have even thought to force Miss Jennings' hand to join with my brother's," he replied, truthfully. "He is not worthy of her."

Lady Mayhew smiled again, her eyes sparkling. "Thank you, Lord Denfield. I admit that I have been rather concerned for my niece but I can see now that I have had no need to be. You possess an excellent character, have a kind heart and gentle spirit. I am sure that you will make Anne very happy indeed."

Peter bowed and took his leave, thanking Lady Mayhew again for what she had told him. As he made his way to the carriage, however, he found himself smiling and, sitting down next to his sister, thought himself very satisfied indeed.

Chapter Eleven

"You are engaged?"

Anne nodded, looking into Lady Grace's astonished face. "I am."

"When I first heard that, I was not entirely sure I believed it which is why I wrote to you," Lady Grace replied, reaching across to grasp Anne's hand as they rode in the carriage together. "And to hear it from your own lips now is most extraordinary!"

Anne managed a slight smile, her own feelings on the matter still a little confused. "Lord Denfield appears to be a good sort of gentleman."

"I am sure that he is for I have never heard any gossip about him," her friend replied, soothing Anne's worries a little more. "It is his brother, Viscount Henley, who is to be avoided."

It is a little late for that, Anne thought to herself, her lips twitching. "So I have heard."

"And tell me, how did this take place?" Lady Grace's eyes were still wide with astonishment. "I heard that he proposed at a ball!"

Anne pressed her lips together, wondering if she dared tell her friend the truth, only to decide that it was best to keep that hidden for the moment. While she considered Lady Grace a friend, she was all too aware that Lady Grace did enjoy listening to gossip and, worse, sharing in it and thus, she chose to keep the truth back from her friend. "He and I both seek a match of simplicity and practicality," she said, honestly. "That has brought us together."

"But you have not courted?"

Anne shook her head. "No, we have not."

"And yet you are engaged?"

Spreading her hands, Anne smiled. "I am aware that it is not the usual way one goes about finding oneself a husband or wife but it suits us both very well, I think."

Lady Grace shook her head and then looked out of the window. "I do not think that I should be pleased with an arrangement such as that," she said, softly. "No, I am quite determined to fall in love."

"Love?" Anne repeated, surprised at how her friend spoke

with such feeling. "I did not think that you would even *consider* such a thing."

"Why not?" Lady Grace looked back at her with a small smile. "Emotion and affection is important to me. I should like to have some sort of feeling for my husband and I should very much like him to feel the same for me! To be practical is one thing but to be loved is quite another!"

Anne considered this, a little surprised to find a stab of longing for such a thing in her own heart. "I think that I shall be satisfied with a kind, respectful husband," she said, forcing herself to believe her own words rather than listen to the whisper in her heart. "Lord Denfield appears to be both of those things."

"Which are admirable qualities to be sure but they do not speak of a gentleman's *heart.*"

"That is true," Anne admitted, softly, her forehead lining as she let herself consider what her friend had said. Thus far, she had never imagined what it would mean to fall in love or to have love in one's heart for a gentleman but clearly, it was something that Lady Grace both considered and wanted. "But alas, I did not have much opportunity to even think of such a thing, such was the haste of our engagement." Realizing she had said a little too much, given the astonished look on Lady Grace's face, Anne flushed gently and looked away. "It is only to say that our engagement was rather quick but given that I *must* marry this Season, it did seem wise to accept him given that he does appear to be an amiable sort."

"Why must you marry this Season?"

Anne laughed ruefully. "Do you not know that I am close enough to be a spinster?" she asked, seeing Lady Grace's eyes round. "My father has quite despaired of me, I am afraid. This was – and is – to be my last Season and I would not be given further opportunity."

Lady Grace tossed her head. "I think that foolishness. One's age ought not to determine one's future. You could be a very contented spinster and *still* find yourself falling in love and marrying, albeit a little later in life than others." Smiling, she reached across and squeezed Anne's hand. "But if *you* are contented, then I am contented also. As I have said, Lord Denfield should be a good husband though I do not know if he has any considerations as regards his heart."

Anne smiled back at her friend, finding Lady Grace both refreshing and unorthodox. Not every young lady would say such things as that. Not every young lady would even imagine that a spinster might still find happiness! Mayhap she could trust her with the truth about what had really taken place.

"Now, you must tell me what your plans for your wedding day are." Lady Grace beamed at her. "I am sure that everyone in the *ton* will be eager to find out what is taking place!"

Anne winced inwardly but forced a smile. "I do not want there to be a large or ostentatious event," she said, slowly, "and neither does Lord Denfield. That is all that has been discussed at present, however. We have a date in mind but there is still a great deal to be done and Lord Denfield must get the license also." A little worried, she looked back into Lady Grace's face steadily. "Are you quite certain that all of the *ton* will wish to hear about my wedding?"

"Why, of course they shall!" Lady Grace laughed, shaking her head as though Anne was being quite ridiculous. "All of the ladies of London enjoy a wedding and knowing some of the details in advance is something that they might talk about amongst themselves. Though I shall say nothing if you do not wish me to."

Swallowing, Anne looked out of the window. Deep down, her fear was that, despite the fact neither her aunt nor she would write to her father to inform him about the upcoming wedding, somehow he would still hear about it, march to London and demand it all come to an end. "I – I should not like anyone to gossip about my wedding."

Lady Grace leaned forward again. "What troubles you so, my dear?"

Anne turned her attention back to her, wondering if she dare be entirely honest. In the end, she decided that she could be and thus, let out a slow breath and lifted her shoulders. "My father is not someone with a kind heart. I have borne the brunt of his criticism and his anger for a long time. My two sisters are already married, though they are younger than I, and when Netty's wedding was over, my father declared that there was an end to things and I would remain a spinster."

Lady Grace's eyes flared in shock.

"My aunt insisted that I attend London with her and be given a final opportunity, though with *her* guidance rather than my father's."

"And it seems to have done you very well!"

Anne smiled. "Yes, it has," she admitted, realizing now how much more at ease she was with her connection to Lord Denfield. "Though my fear at present is that, if my father hears of my engagement, he may attempt to prevent it."

The shock returned to Lady Grace's face. "But why?"

"Because my aunt believes that he would prefer to me to remain a spinster so that he might make use of me for his own benefit. I could run the house for him, take on duties instead of him and – "

"Become a drudge."

Anne nodded sadly. "Yes, that is precisely what I think. Though I cannot yet prove it, of course and it may be that, should he hear of it, he will do nothing other than be irritated about it while remaining at home but my aunt is concerned and, therefore, I am concerned with her."

"I see." Lady Grace bit her lip. "I am much too inclined towards gossip, Miss Jennings, I admit but I will do my best to make certain that any such gossip is quelled before it can take hold. You need not tell me anything about your wedding if you do not wish to."

"It is not that I do not trust you," Anne protested at once, only for Lady Grace to laugh and shake her head.

"My dear lady, I do not trust myself! My tongue is much too loose." She smiled gently. "Though I am glad that you trusted me enough to tell me about your father. I give you my word that I will not breathe even a hint about this to any other. I can see that it is a delicate subject though I am sorry that you have been faced with so much."

Anne lifted her shoulders and let them fall. "I have Aunt Mayhew now. It is not as bad as it might have been and I am very grateful indeed for her company and her guidance, as I am for your friendship."

Lady Grace smiled broadly and sat back in her seat. "As am I, Miss Jennings."

***

80

"Here now, is this not a fine spot?"

Anne smiled and sat down beside her friend, glad to know that Lady Grace's mother was nearby. She had taken lunch with a friend but had now met them both at St James's Park, ready to chaperone them both as they sat for their picnic.

"It is a very fine spot, yes." Anne smiled and looked all around her. "There are so very few people out walking which is not at all what I had expected. I thought the park might be full of gentlemen and ladies all taking in the sunshine."

Lady Grace laughed. "Except you forget that genteel ladies are not meant to have even a single freckle upon their nose so most of them will do their utmost to stay inside when the sun is at its highest."

Anne, who had always known such a thing but had thought it a little ridiculous the length some ladies had gone to protect their ivory skin, laughed along with Lady Grace, glad indeed to find that they were kindred spirits in this regard also. "I certainly do have a parasol but it is not something I am inclined to take out very often."

"Though now that you are to be wed, I suppose such things do not matter a great deal," Lady Grace teased, as Anne smiled softly. "I, however, ought to be much more careful than I am. Thankfully, my mother has quite given up on me now so I can do whatever I wish!"

Making to say something more, Anne was interrupted by a shout which, having caught her attention at the first, soon made her gasp with shock. A gentleman was striding across the grass towards them both, his hands tight by his sides, his frame stiff and when she looked up at him, his face dark with what she thought was anger. It was only when he drew closer that she realized the darkness she saw in his expression was *not* only just the shadows of his upset but rather bruised skin.

"Lord Henley." All of a sudden, the calm that she felt, the quiet in her spirit and the happiness she had shared with Lady Grace evaporated. Instead, she found herself twisted up inside with worry over what he might do next, with what he might say to her even though she was in company. After all, that had not mattered before so why would it matter to him now? She licked her lips, unable to find something to else to say while Lord Henley simply stood there, glaring down at her.

"I hear you are engaged to my brother now."

Anne nodded but said nothing, hearing a rustling of skirts beside her. Lady Grace rose to her feet and Anne chose to do so also, aware of how quickly her heart was beating as Lord Henley's brow furrowed.

"Do you see the damage you've done to me?" he exclaimed, gesturing to his bruised face. "Had you not decided to pull back from what was meant only as a bit of fun, then this would never have happened! Though you have gained very prettily from it, I suppose."

Seeing Lady Grace's curious look, Anne lifted her chin and, balling her hands into fists, attempted to speak with a confidence which usually evaded her. "This is your own doing, Lord Henley. Your attentions were unwelcome."

"My doing? *You* were the one who stepped back, who practically threw me to the ground!"

Anne shook her head and pressed her lips together, not certain what else she should say. Lord Henley's face was something of a mess, she had to admit. There were streaks of blue running under his eyes, with green and purple across his cheeks. His bridge of his nose was swollen with an obvious cut across the center of it and, had Anne been in Lord Henley's position, she would not have even thought to step out in society.

"I do think that you are being rather dramatic." Lady Grace rolled her eyes obviously as she took a step closer to Anne. "In looking at you, I cannot imagine that Lady Anne thought to knock you to the ground. She would not have the strength!"

This seemed to take some of the wind out of Lord Henley's sails for he opened his mouth to say something more – no doubt to give a retort – only to close it again. His eyes, however, remained narrowed.

"I hold this lady entirely responsible for the damage done to me," he declared, lifting his chin but keeping his gaze fixed to Anne. "I am the subject of amusement and ridicule in the esteemed circles of London! Everywhere I go, there are people mocking me, teasing me because of my appearance!"

"Which I am sorry to hear of but that does not mean that

82

you can place the responsibility for *your* accident upon my shoulders," Anne replied, a little surprised at the sheer amount of strength she was able to summon in speaking so directly to Lord Henley. "We do not need to argue, however. We are to be family soon enough, are we not?"

Instead of taking a hold of this kindness, instead of accepting the chance to put all of this to one side and leave things be, Lord Henley's lip curled as he sneered at her. "I have no intention of treating you – or even considering you – family, Miss Jennings. You will, no doubt, be just as my brother and sister are in *their* condemnation of me and therefore, I have no desire to set aside our argument or consider you as family to me. We shall be at odds, Miss Jennings and I shall continue to hold you responsible for the damage to my features. Good day!"

Anne took a step back as Lord Henley swept away, his back straight, his chin still lifted. It was not until Lady Grace took her hand in her own that she realized she had been staring at him.

"I will not pretend that I understand everything that Lord Henley said to you but it certainly appears as though he is deeply displeased."

"Because that is all he is," Anne answered, making to sit back down on the picnic blanket. Her heart was still hammering rather painfully and she closed her eyes briefly before trying to smile at her friend, who gave her nothing more than a concerned look. "I must beg of you not to tell anyone what you overheard, Lady Grace." Seeing her friend nod, Anne took in a deep breath and tried to find a sense of calmness within herself. "If you wish, I shall tell you everything but you must swear to me that you will not speak a word of it to anyone else."

Lady Grace's eyes rounded but she nodded quickly, her hands going together in a prayer position. "Of course, Miss Jennings. We are friends, are we not? And I would say nothing which would injure a friend."

"I thank you." Closing her eyes again, Anne drank in clean, sweet air and then, opening her eyes, spread her hands wide. "Then I shall start at the beginning."

Chapter Twelve

"Miss Jennings has come to call, my lord."

Peter almost fell out of his chair in his hurry to get to his feet and thereafter, to the door. "Miss Jennings? Where?"

"In the parlour with Lady Symington who arrived at the very same time. Miss Jennings stated she can only stay for a few minutes as she is without a chaperone."

Nodding – though he did wonder where her aunt might be – Peter hurried out of the room and made his way directly to the parlor. The delight he felt at the thought of seeing Miss Jennings again was rather surprising and though he let it fill his heart, he wondered at it still. With it, however, came a fear that she was suddenly going to pull their engagement apart and, as he considered that for just a moment, Peter again was overcome with the astonishment of just how much he did not desire such a thing. They had only been engaged for a few days, the *ton* had only just recovered from the shock of learning of their impending marriage and yet, his dedication to their engagement seemed to be very steadfast indeed!

"Miss Jennings?" Hurrying into the parlor, he stopped only to bow before coming closer, seeing her eyes meet his. "Is there something wrong?"

She smiled quickly with Julia waving a hand, urging him silently to sit down. "No, not wrong, Lord Denfield."

"But there is something troubling you."

Miss Jennings nodded as Peter eased himself into a chair, seeing how Julia's eyes lingered on Miss Jennings, clearly feeling the same concern as he.

"I was enjoying a picnic with a friend in St James's Park this afternoon," Miss Jennings began, glancing from Peter to Julia and back again, "with her mother playing chaperone for us both. Something took place and though I did not want to speak of it to you, Lady Grace insisted that I do so."

"Lady Grace?" Peter inquired.

"My friend," Miss Jennings answered, her face a little pink in her cheeks. "We were talking together only for Lord Henley to spy us."

In an instant, dread broke over Peter's head like a rolling thundercloud, making his heart sink low as he closed his eyes for a moment. If Henley was involved then he had no doubt that whatever Miss Jennings had endured, it would have been by his brother's hand.

"What happened?" Julia asked, her voice soft with concern. "I do hope he did nothing untoward."

"He... he did speak to me," came the slightly stammered reply, with Miss Jennings now lacing and unlacing her fingers. "His face was something of a mess of bruises."

Peter snorted, shaking his head. "That is entirely his own doing. He ought not to have done what he did to you, Miss Jennings and had he refrained, then I am sure that his face would, at this moment, be perfectly intact."

She gave him a small, wane smile which Peter returned, though his worry over what Henley had done lingered near to the edge of his mind.

"He states that he blames me for the injury to his nose," Miss Jennings said slowly, now not looking at either Peter or at Julia but rather letting her gaze fall – and linger – on her hands. "He stated it quite clearly. I did suggest that we need not argue since we were to be family but he told me that he has no intention of treating me or even viewing me as family." Her head lifted, her green eyes glistening just a little and Peter's heart swelled with anger over his brother's actions. "I did not know what to do or what to say so, in truth, I simply decided to let him say whatever he wished before attempting to cajole him again."

"Which failed, I am sure."

A hint of a smile touched the corner of Miss Jennings' lips. "I did not have opportunity for he was quite clear that he had said all that he needed to say and thereafter, took his leave of me." Her lips pressed tight together again. "I do not mean to trouble you with this but nor do I want to be considered as one responsible for the injury to your brother."

Peter's eyebrows lifted. "And you think that I would consider you responsible, Miss Jennings?"

Her brow furrowed. "I do not think that you do, Lord Denfield, but I am a little concerned that the *ton* might believe it. And I cannot have word of my engagement making its way... out of

London."

Recalling what Miss Jennings was speaking of was related to her father and quickly remembering all that Lady Mayhew had spoken to him about, Peter let out a slow breath of relief, seeing now where the lady's concern had come from.

"That is not because I have any concerns about our engagement," she said quickly, her face now coloring. "Please understand, I do not wish to step away from our engagement nor do I wish to hide it from anyone, it is – "

"Please do not concern yourself." Peter smiled gently, seeing how her eyes became watchful, perhaps uncertain as to what he meant. "Your aunt has already spoken to me about certain things."

Miss Jennings blinked rapidly. "She has?"

"She has. It was said out of concern for you and I fully understand that there is no requirement for me to speak to or write to your father about our engagement. After all, you are of age, are you not?"

Her face flushed all the redder. "I am, yes."

Peter's smile grew. "Then we are quite at ease and understanding, Miss Jennings."

Miss Jennings held his gaze for a long moment and then, after a short while, let out a slow breath and closed her eyes for just a second before opening them again. When she looked to him, the smile on her face grew all over again, though there was a relief within it which made his heart soften.

"I thank you, Lord Denfield." Miss Jennings rose from her chair and Peter quickly followed after her, bowing as she dropped into a quick curtsy. "I should take my leave now. My aunt will be expecting my return."

"But of course." Peter offered to accompany her to the door but she smiled and told him she would be quite well able to do so herself before walking from the room and closing the door behind her.

Peter sat back down into his chair and let out a huff of breath, his brows knotting and his jaw tight. He did not much like what it was that his brother had done to Miss Jennings and was all the more ashamed that she had been a little frightened because of it. It was a dark and desperate thing to frighten a lady so and Peter was upset because of it.

"What is it about Miss Jennings' father that is so concerning?"

Peter looked to his sister, having forgotten that she was still here, given that he had been so lost in his thoughts. "Miss Jennings' father, Lord Ellon, would prefer that she remain a spinster."

Julia's eyes rounded as she snatched in a breath.

"It is for his own selfish reasons, of course," Peter told her, with a small shrug. "Lady Mayhew has made it perfectly clear that Lord Ellon is nothing more than a brute, who has not only driven Miss Jennings' mother away out of fear and dread, but has also thought to keep Miss Jennings' for his own benefit. That is to say, he thinks to make her a drudge, to do as he wishes and to run the household for him so that he might have a life of comfort."

"But that is dreadful! Does not every father wish for their children to have happiness in their future?"

"It is generally presumed that they do but in this case, it appears that Miss Jennings does not have such a gentleman for a father. She is clearly afraid that, if news of our engagement were to reach her father, he would do his utmost to bring it to an end before we could marry."

Julia shook her head, clicking her tongue. "That is dreadful. Though it does require that we do whatever we can to prevent Henley from continuing to behave as he is."

Peter pursed his lips and thought for a few moments before shaking his head. "I do not know what I am to do about Henley."

"Nor do I, unfortunately." Julia let out a sigh and looked away, her frown growing. "If I possessed the fortitude, I would administer a thorough admonishment to him until he ultimately regained his senses."

Despite the seriousness of their conversation, Peter could not help but laugh as Julia glanced back at him, her face a little pink though she smiled somewhat ruefully at him.

A knock at the door interrupted his thoughts and, calling the servant to come in, he scowled the very moment that a particular person walked through the door.

Lord Henley's messenger.

"You come with a message from my brother," Peter stated, as the man dropped his head, his hands hanging by his sides.

"What is it that he wishes me to do this time?"

The man cleared his throat and clasped his hands behind his back and, for a moment, Peter found himself feeling a little sympathetic for the fellow. After all, it was not his fault that Henley was sending him to Peter again and again, was it?

"Lord Henley begs of you to bring the carriage to Wilson Street, for he has found himself with such a headache, he cannot move from his chair."

"And why could you not go to fetch his own carriage?" Peter asked, though the man merely glanced at him and then dropped his head again. With a hiss of breath, Peter pushed himself up in his chair but caught Julia's swift shake of the head, reminding him that he was not meant to be going to his brother's aid simply because it was requested. "You may inform Lord Henley that I am indisposed and unable to come to Wilson Street at the present moment."

The man looked up again at Peter and then dropped his head, giving a small nod which, Peter presumed, was in agreement with what had been said. The urging of his heart told Peter to take back what had been said, to go in search of his brother and to take him back home so he might recover but the reminder of Miss Jennings' pale face and hearing the words on her lips as regarded his brother's actions towards her kept him from doing so.

"Lord Kettlebridge is in Wilson Street," Julia mused aloud as the man took his leave of Peter. "He is often in our brother's company."

"And has very fine French brandy," Peter replied with a small sigh. "Though I have no doubt that our brother's head truly does pain him, given all that has taken place of late."

Julia shook her head. "And he will have added to his pain by his own foolishness."

"No doubt."

His sister looked at him curiously. "You still wish to go to him, do you not?"

Peter nodded, seeing no reason to hide the truth from his sister. "Of course I do. I have always cared for Henley and for you. You are wed, settled and happy and I fear now that Henley will never be so. If he continues to live in this way then all that will greet him one day will be emptiness and solitude. I had thought – I had hoped – that if I were to continue to aid him, he might see the foolishness of his ways and would wish to become a truly respectable gentleman but, more and more, I see him continuing down this path of foolishness."

"As do I," Julia admitted, heavily. "But what can be done?"

"Nothing more," Peter replied, his whole being sorrowful. "We have all tried and nothing has changed. He has become worse, even speaking to Miss Jennings as he did! I will have to talk to him about that. He *cannot* continue in this way." With a scowl, he shook his head. "I will have to be a little heavier in my words and in my demands, I think."

Julia looked at him, her eyebrows low over her eyes. "What do you think to do?"

"I am not certain yet," Peter acknowledged, "but I am fully determined that Henley will not speak to Miss Jennings in such a way again." A sense of protectiveness crashed over him and he lifted his chin. "Never again."

Chapter Thirteen

Anne looked all around the room, trying to smile despite the nervousness which still clawed at her heart. Even though she had spoken to Lord Denfield and, thereafter, her aunt about what had taken place with Lord Henley, that sense of unease had not left her. What if he was here this evening? What if he came up to her again, in front of all those who watched her, and began to berate her all over again? What would she do? It would not be as though she would be easily able to find something to say in response!

"Now, do try not to look so nervous." Lady Mayhew smiled at her as Anne looked at her, aware now that her expression was obviously one of concern. "I will be by your side this entire evening – unless you are dancing, of course – and will make certain that Lord Henley does not come anywhere near to you. And, if he should somehow manage to do so, then *I* will be the one speaking to him rather than you." A glint came into her eye. "I can assure you that once *I* speak with him, he will not dare come near you again."

This made Anne smile. "I am certain that is true."

"Then do not look so worried! Enjoy this evening. I am sure your dance card will be filled within the hour."

Anne clasped her hands together and pressed her lips tight flat. She did not have the same confidence as her aunt but perhaps, given that her engagement was now well known by everyone within the *ton,* she might have a slightly improved chance of being asked to dance. Not that such a thing mattered now, given that she was already engaged. *Though I should like to dance with Lord Denfield.*

That thought sent her heart clamoring furiously as she closed her eyes and tried to steady herself. After she had spoken to Lord Denfield the previous afternoon, she had sensed such a kindness and sweetness about his character that her heart had lurched towards him with such a strength, her breath had been quite stolen away for a few moments. She had not given herself much time to consider that reaction as yet but the more she thought of it, the more she began to realize just how much her heart was beginning to feel for Lord Denfield. There was a contentment in her heart when she thought of herself engaged to him, a happiness, almost, that was continuing to grow in strength. To know that she would soon be his wife and that she would have a husband who was kind, considerate and generous was a great blessing and not one that she could ever turn from.

"Miss Jennings, good evening!"

Anne was pulled from her thoughts as she smiled quickly at Lady Grace, seeing how bright and excited her eyes were. "Lady Grace, good evening."

"I do hope you are well?" Lady Grace's eyes suddenly rounded with obvious concern. "After yesterday afternoon's conflict with Lord Henley, I confess that I found myself worrying about your state of mind."

Anne smiled quickly, wanting to put her friend at ease. "I did as you suggested and spoke with Lord Denfield about the matter. I thought I would only stand in the hallway and speak to him given that I had no chaperone but Lady Symington was present and so we all sat together."

Lady Grace nodded, though her eyes remained fixed on Anne. "And was he helpful? Did he take what you had to say with any seriousness?"

"With all seriousness," Anne confirmed, seeing the relief etch itself into Lady Grace's face. "Surely you could not expect him to do anything else?"

A quiet chuckle escaped from her friend. "My dear lady, I do not know what I should think! I do not know the gentleman particularly well though I did think him of good character, so I am glad indeed that you found him so willing to listen."

"As was I. Though I did sense there was embarrassment on his part, which I did not want him to feel."

"That is to be expected," her aunt chimed in, as Lady Grace nodded. "He is the head of the family, therefore whatever family disgrace there is will cast a shadow upon him also."

Anne's heart twisted with a sudden sympathy for Lord Denfield, though her consideration of his character grew all the stronger. How glad she was now that he had stepped in to engage himself to her rather than forcing her to wed his brother!

"Lady Grace, Miss Jennings." A gentleman Anne struggled to place bowed before them both, a broad smile on his face as he lifted his head. "How excellent to spy you both together! It means that I do not have to trouble myself to run around and around the ballroom in the hope of finding you."

"And why do you wish to find us, Lord Charleston?" Lady Grace asked, as Lord Charleston grinned, perhaps hearing the same teasing note in her voice as Anne heard also.

"So that I might have the pleasure of requesting your dance cards," Lord Charleston replied, with a broad smile on his face. "I should very much like to stand up with you both."

Anne glanced to her aunt but Lady Mayhew was already conversing with an acquaintance, clearly quite contented with Lord Charleston's presence. With a nod, she slipped her dance card from her wrist and handed it to Lord Charleston, making him beam with pleasure. Lady Grace threw Anne a smile, though she quickly returned her gaze to Lord Charleston.

"And might I have the pleasure of taking your dance card from you thereafter?"

Anne turned her attention to the approaching gentleman only for her to snatch in her breath as Lord Henley inclined his head towards her. She did not know what to say, for she could not easily refuse him in front of Lord Charleston yet, at the very same time, the last thing she wanted to do was stand up with Lord Henley.

"I am sure these two fine ladies will have no complaint in that regard," Lord Charleston chortled, clearly entirely unaware of the difficulties Anne would have with this gentleman as he handed Lord Henley Anne's dance card. "Though I must ask, Lord Henley, if you are in a fit state to dance?"

Lord Henley offered him a small, rather tight smile and Lady Grace's features twisted as she took in his black eyes and injury to his nose. Anne swallowed hard, looking to Lady Grace again as her friend threw her another look.

"I am quite able to dance," he said, tightly. "My hands and feet are not injured in any way."

Anne, who still had a few bruises from what Lord Henley had done in attempting to kiss her, found herself lifting her chin and looking the gentleman straight in the eye, suddenly a little irritated by the gentleman's determination to press in upon her life. "That makes one of us, Lord Henley."

Lord Charleston was too busy looking at Lady Grace's dance card to offer her remark any particular attention but Lord Henley clearly understood what it was that she meant, given the way he scowled.

"I do not think I should like to dance, I am afraid," Anne continued, marveling within herself at the confidence she was able to suddenly summon. "I am to be very cautious about which gentlemen I stand up with for fear that some might step on my toes and fall into me or some other thing. Therefore, Lord Henley, I should be much appreciative if you could refrain." Despite the confidence which had come in her speaking, Anne did not feel at all at ease in his company, her stomach immediately beginning to twist this way and that, her hands clasped tightly in front of her as she forced herself to keep her gaze steady upon his face. Lord Henley's expression grew ugly and he took a small step closer to her, making Anne instantly desire to step back from him though, with an effort, she remained exactly where she was.

"I am doing my level best to apologise, though such things are not particularly well known to me," he said, rather gruffly. "Do you not understand, Miss Jennings? This is my way of attempting to make amends between us."

Anne blinked in surprise, though her heart warned her not to immediately believe him.

"My brother has spoken to me about my behaviour and, truthfully, I did not realise how much my actions would have brought you fear," he continued, though his dark expression did not change in the least. "I should like to dance with you so that we may put an end to the strain and tension between us."

Her heart still clamored with warning not to believe Lord Henley though she said nothing of the sort to him. What was she to do? Could there be any way in which she might find herself trusting his words?

"I truly am sorry for all that I have done." Lord Henley put one hand to his heart and bowed his head. "I have behaved atrociously towards you and for that, there can be nothing worse that hearing me merely saying that I am sorry and being able to do nothing more to improve it. However, I will state how glad I am that you are to marry my brother, for he is an excellent fellow and you will, I am sure, be very contented with him. Though, of course,

I ought not to have done what I attempted to do in the first place, in which this situation would, therefore, never have arisen in the first place."

Anne swallowed hard, her anxiety about his nearness to her beginning to fade. Could it be that he spoke truthfully here? Or was she right still to doubt him?

"My brother has always been the sort to care for me," Lord Henley continued, when she said nothing. "He has made it plain, now, that he will no longer come to my assistance or to my aid whenever I find myself in difficulty. That is not something that I ought to blame him for, however, given that he is doing such a thing simply to prove that *I* must bear the consequences of my actions upon myself from now on. I confess that I have begun to see how dark and cruel a person I have become. I do seek to rectify these things, Miss Jennings, and I do so now, beginning with you so that I might apologise to you for my actions."

"I see," Anne squeaked, a little uncertain as to what she ought to do or say. "That is... very gracious of you, Lord Henley."

"It is the very least I can do." He bowed again and then looked expectantly at her dance card. "Might you permit me this, Miss Jennings? Might you permit me to step out with you for one day? I promise I shall not take the waltz for I am sure you wish very much for my brother to step in there. In fact, shall I not write his initials upon the card for him? I am a little surprised he has not appeared as yet, though no doubt, when he does, he will wish to speak only with you."

Anne could say nothing, could *do* nothing other than watch Lord Henley write Lord Denfield's initials down on the waltz and, thereafter, turn his gaze to hers. "and I shall write mine in the quadrille, if you will permit me?"

What was she to say? She wanted very much to refuse him, to tell him that no, she did not want to dance the quadrille with him, did not want anything particular to do with him but with the *ton* nearby and Lady Grace and Lord Charleston standing nearby, it seemed she had no choice.

"I think, Lord Henley, that I should prefer it if – "

"Henley? Whatever are you doing here?"

Before Anne could finish speaking, before Lord Henley could say another word, Lord Denfield put one hand to Anne's arm and, stepping in front of her, came face to face with his brother.

"I am writing my name down for the quadrille, brother," came the reply. "That is all." Anne watched helplessly as Lord Henley wrote his name there before she could even ask him to refrain. "And I have already placed your name in the waltz."

Lord Denfield looked immediately to Anne, though he had no choice but to lift her shoulders and let them fall, trying to communicate with him that she had not desired this but that Lord Henley had chosen to do so regardless. Lord Denfield's frown began to grow and he then gestured to the dance card. "May I?"

"Of course. As I have said, I have already placed your name on the waltz, for I was sure that you would wish to step out with your betrothed."

Lord Denfield glanced again at Anne and then nodded. "But of course. And the polka as well, if you wish?"

Anne could only smile though this quickly faded as she gave Lord Henley another glance. For whatever reason, he was smiling at her, though there was a glint in his eye she did not like. Indeed, it was as though his lip curled rather than smiled, as though he were doing something in this moment that she was not aware of, that he was achieving his own purposes through this game he played. She shuddered lightly as his eyes narrowed just a fraction before, chuckling, he inclined his head.

"I shall take my leave of you both," he said, leaving Anne to stand with Lord Denfield as they both watched him wind his way through the crowd in the ballroom. Letting out a slow breath of relief, Anne turned her attention back to Lord Denfield who was frowning heavily.

"I do not understand what he is doing," he said, quietly. "You say that he approached you?"

Anne nodded. "He did. He apologised for his previous behaviour and told me that he very much wishes for there to be an improvement in such things. I confess that I did not know whether or not I should believe him and I do apologise for that. I – "

"You need not apologise," came the quick reply. "I quite understand your concern. I did speak to my brother last evening, however."

Anne's eyebrows lifted. "You did?"

Lord Denfield nodded. "We had something of a

disagreement. He sent a messenger to ask for my aid and I refused to go to him. It was not something that he was expecting, I do not think, for though I have been behaving so of late, perhaps the fact that he has a slight injury might have made him believe I would be more considerate of him."

Turning to face Lord Denfield a little more, Anne looked into his face, seeing the steadiness in his eyes but the lines across his forehead, speaking of confusion.

"When he returned – and once he had sobered a little – he grew angry with me for my lack of consideration. In response, I spoke to him at length about his behaviour, though this is not the first time such things have been brought to his attention! Eventually, we parted though I confess that I did not believe that a single word I had said made a single bit of difference to him. I thought that he had ignored every word I spoke and had made it quite clear that I was not to speak of his behaviour to him again." Pausing, Lord Denfield shook his head. "Though mayhap I was wrong. It is not like my brother to speak to anyone about what he has done and certainly even *less* like him to apologise!"

Anne nodded, turning her eyes in Lord Henley's direction again though he had, by now, quite disappeared into the crowd. "I can see that."

"Though I am glad that he has done," Lord Denfield said quickly. "You did not wish to dance with him, I think."

Offering Lord Denfield a slightly wry smile, Anne spread her hands. "I did say that I had no desire to step out with him but that was before he apologised. And then, though I had not given him my consent, he did write his name there. Perhaps he thought that I would be willing to step out with him because of his apology."

Lord Denfield winced. "Yet again, he forces his presence upon you."

"But you will watch us both, I am sure," Anne said quickly, hoping that Lord Denfield would quickly assent, which he did. "I confess that I am still rather concerned. I do hope that does not make you think ill of me."

A smile quickly spread across Lord Denfield's face and his hand squeezed hers suddenly, making her heart warm with a sudden, fresh happiness which seemed to push away all that she feared in one single moment. "But of course it does not. If I am to be truthful, Miss Jennings, I am pleased that you are able to speak so openly with me. It stands us in good stead, I think."

Anne blinked quickly, realizing that what Lord Denfield said was quite true. She had spoken to him without hesitating, had been truthful with him about her heart and her feelings when she had expected to struggle. It seemed that the closer they grew, the more time they spent together, the easier it was for her to speak with him – and that could only be a delightful thing.

Do I have an affection for him? her heart questioned, as she pulled her gaze away, realizing that she was smiling without really thinking about it. *Or is it merely a gentle respect?*

"Now, the polka is the next dance, I believe." Lord Denfield interrupted her thoughts by offering her his arm, smiling down into her eyes. "Shall we, Miss Jennings?"

"But of course, Lord Denfield." Accepting his arm, Anne returned his smile and then made her way to the floor, finding herself walking with such happiness, it forced a smile to her face that she could not push away. She would not think of Lord Henley, she decided, as she stepped back from Lord Denfield so she might curtsy, as was expected of the dance. Instead, she would focus all of her attentions upon Lord Denfield for slowly but surely, this gentleman was taking a firm grip upon her heart.

Chapter Fourteen

"I do not know what he is doing, Symington."

Lord Symington shrugged. "Might he be truthful?"

Instantly, Peter shook his head. "No, I do not think so. I know my brother and I confess that I am afraid that what he is doing at present has another motive."

"You mean to say that he is not in the least bit apologetic? That he has no intention of changing his ways?"

Peter nodded. "Precisely that."

"But why would he do such a thing? What purpose would there be in it?"

Biting the edge of his lip, Peter shook his head and then did not answer for some moments. There was something about his brother's behavior both towards Miss Jennings and to himself that did not sit well with him. "When I finished my argument with my brother the day before the ball – the day that Miss Jennings came to speak with me about what he had done and said in approaching her in the park – he was so angry with me, he roared that he wished I would simply forget I even had a brother so that I would not bother him any more. To go from that to a gentleman who is willing not only to apologise but to appease is not at all what I expected of him."

"I see."

Peter's lips twisted as Lord Symington and he walked through the park together. "I am determined to keep the truth about Lord Ellon from his ears. I fear that, should he learn that Miss Jennings has asked to keep her engagement from her father, he might do the very opposite of what she desires."

Lord Symington nodded, having heard about this from Julia. "That is wise, at least." His head tilted. "What about Miss Jennings' mother? Where is she?"

"I – " Peter frowned, his words cut short. "I am afraid I do not know. I recall Lady Mayhew saying something about her but I do not quite remember. What I *do* remember is that she is not, at present, living at the Ellon estate but elsewhere. Lady Mayhew said something about Lord Ellon being something of a dislikeable fellow and I do wonder what effect his nature has had upon his wife."

Lord Symington sighed and shook his head. "It is an evil gentleman who treats his wife and daughters with any sort of cruelty."

"Indeed," Peter murmured, a sharp sympathy stabbing through his heart. "I do wonder if Lady Mayhew would wish to invite her to the wedding, however?"

"You could but ask. In fact, I think it would show Miss Jennings that you care not only about her but also about her family if you were to ask her about her mother."

Peter mused on this for a few moments, then nodded. "Yes, I think that would be a wise idea."

"Then you admit it?" Lord Symington's voice was light. "You *do* care for Miss Jennings?"

Coming to an immediate stop, Peter stared at his friend, then snorted, rolled his eyes and continued on his way. "I am concerned for her, if that is what you mean."

"That is *not* what I mean and well you know it," came the teasing response. "There is a softness in your heart when it comes to the lady."

Peter considered this but then shrugged. "I would say I have a sympathy for her."

"There is more than that, surely?" his friend exclaimed, eyes wide. "You must feel more than sympathy when you dance with her."

Peter opened his mouth to say that he did not, only to recall how he had felt when he had swept Miss Jennings up into a waltz. There had been more than sympathy there, certainly. He had felt himself almost eager to grow closer to her, desiring to pull her a little more tightly into his arms. Where had that come from if it was not from his heart?

"You see?" Lord Symington chuckled, tapping the side of his nose with one finger. "I knew that there was something more there."

"I am not saying that there is or is not," Peter retorted, though his friend only grinned. "It is not something that I have considered."

"Though it is a very good thing if you *do* care for her," Lord Symington continued, quickly. "For a gentleman to care for his wife makes for a very contented marriage, I think."

99

Peter cleared his throat and was about to say more, only for his gaze to fall upon none other than the very lady they had been speaking about. She was walking arm in arm with another young lady – a young lady that Peter quickly recognized to be his sister. "I did not think that Julia intended to join us this afternoon."

Lord Symington only shrugged. "She was walking with Lady Henstridge and evidently, upon her return, spied your betrothed! What a capital thing!"

"Very," Peter replied, a little dryly as he silently wondered whether his sister had anticipated this and done such a thing on purpose, though that idea quickly threw itself from his mind as he realized that Julia must have come across Miss Jennings quite by chance. After all, it was not as though they had arranged it.

"Just look who I came upon!" Julia's first words confirmed what Peter had been thinking. "Lady Mayhew is a little ways behind us, though she is coming to join us all. Lady Leitway spied her and took her arm, just as I took the arm of Miss Jennings!"

"How very fortunate." Peter inclined his head and smiled as Miss Jennings bobbed a curtsy, surprised at how elated his heart felt upon seeing the lady. "Good afternoon, Miss Jennings. Might I be able to steal you from my sister? We could walk back towards your aunt, if that should please you."

"But of course." Miss Jennings smiled her thanks to Julia and, thereafter came to join Peter, setting her hand on his arm. "Thank you, Lord Denfield."

"I am delighted to have you with me," Peter said, meaning every word. "Now, you may be surprised to know that Lod Symington and I were just discussing you." He began to wander carefully along the path, leaving his sister and her husband to walk together after them. He felt rather than saw the surprise that his statement brought about, given the way that her hand instantly tightened on his arm.

"We were not saying other than praising you," he said quickly, seeing the worry leave her expression at once. "How you have dealt with my brother has been admirable." He offered her a small smile. "How you have dealt with this *all* has been admirable."

"You are very kind."

"Might I... " Remembering the conversation and the suggestion from Lord Symington, he coughed lightly before he continued, trying to gather his thoughts. "Might I ask you some things about your mother?"

"About my mother?" Miss Jennings repeated, sounding surprised. "What is it that you would like to know?"

Peter licked his lips. "I should just like to know about *her*," he said, attempting to explain. "After all, you are to be my wife and I should like to know about the lady I am to call mother-in-law."

Miss Jennings hesitated for a few moments and then, much to his relief, smiled. "You are very kind to ask, Lord Denfield. Of course I should be glad to share a little about her. I think she would be quite delighted in you."

This made Peter flush though he said nothing.

"There is a tension there, however," Miss Jennings continued, quickly. "My mother does not live at my father's estate at present. Indeed, she has not done for some time."

Peter nodded. "Your aunt told me that she is visiting your other aunt in Scotland."

Miss Jennings' smile grew a little weary. "Yes, though she has been visiting for some time. Many months, in fact. It is almost close to a year that she has been away with Lady Stirling."

A little surprised, Peter's eyebrows lifted. "Scotland is some distance away, I suppose."

"She missed my sister's wedding," Miss Jennings sighed, softly. "As I have said, there is a tension here, Lord Denfield. I do not like to admit it but it is best that you know. Mayhap I ought to have told you from the beginning."

"It is not something that you need to hide from me. I do not think that there is any sort of disgrace there, if that is your concern. I... I know enough of your father's character from a distance to have some understanding."

Miss Jennings' eyes closed. "I see." Opening them, she offered him a small smile. "It is best for my mother to be away from him, I think. There can be no happiness when he is present. Do not mistake me, however, he has done his duty as regards finding security for my sisters but – "

"But not for you?"

Her eyes glistened with sudden, unexpected tears. "I was always failing," she replied, hoarsely. "I was always a little below what he was expecting and could never quite reach the standards that my sisters reached."

Peter clicked his tongue, his anger beginning to bubble. "That seems most unfair and I am certain that is entirely untrue also."

Miss Jennings glanced at him. "Mayhap, I believe that the harsh tone he offered me, the heaviness he placed upon me, he also placed upon my mother though, no doubt, to a much sterner degree. Though I miss her terribly, I should say that I am glad she is free of what she has borne for so long. I do not know what she shall do in the future but for the moment, I am contented."

An idea came so quickly into Peter's mind, he caught his breath in a snatch of air, causing Miss Jennings to look at him curiously. He managed a smile, waving her interest away with a shrug of his shoulders. "Thank you for telling me of her, Miss Jennings. Look now, here comes your aunt."

Some conversation followed, with both Lady Mayhew and himself conversing together, though, in the back of his mind, Peter clung to the thought which had come to him during his conversation with Miss Jennings.

The lady cared deeply for her mother, though she had not seen her in some time. Dark circumstances had pushed Lady Ellon away from Lord Ellon *and* from her daughters but surely there was something he could do, a way that he could bring a little light and happiness to Miss Jennings.

Somehow – and mayhap with Lady Mayhew's help – he would be able to bring Lady Ellon to London so she might witness the marriage of her daughter. Would that not make Miss Jennings happy? And was that not just what he wanted for her? The more he thought about it, the more he imagined the delight that Miss Jennings would feel when she laid her eyes upon her mother made his heart sing with hope and expectation... and the realization that yes, he was beginning to care for Miss Jennings in a deeper way than he had ever imagined.

Chapter Fifteen

"I do hope you are enjoying the dinner?"

Anne nodded and smiled at Lady Symington. "Very much, I thank you."

"I am glad. I am also glad that my brother permitted me to have the ladies and gentlemen opposite each other rather than in between for I have very much enjoyed our conversation this evening."

When the invitation had come to join Lord Denfield, Lord and Lady Symington and a few other guests for dinner, Anne had been a little worried that Lord Henley might be present also, though that fear had been brushed away the very moment she had sat down for dinner and seen every seat taken. Lord Henley had either not been invited, or there had been something which had prevented him from joining them all this evening. Either way, she was relieved.

"I do think that this evening has gone *very* well," Lady Symington sighed, looking sidelong at Anne. "I am also glad that Henley was otherwise engaged."

It was as though the lady had known her thoughts and Anne flushed, looking at her friend. "I admit that I too am a little relieved, though I did not like to say so."

"But we already knew it," came the reply. "And it is quite understandable. Henley has not behaved well and, no doubt, is choosing not to do as he ought this evening also, given that he is at some gambling den or other." With a sigh, she looked away. "It is disappointing, I will admit but what can be done? Though I am glad to hear that he apologised to you."

Anne nodded as though to confirm that what Lady Symington said was quite right. "Yes, he did. And we also danced together."

"Though you were not particularly enamoured with the idea, I understand," Lady Symington laughed, shaking her head. "I quite understand *that,* also! I do not know what Henley was thinking though if his apology is genuine, then that is an excellent thing, if not a little surprising."

Anne said nothing, lapsing into silence and considering all

that her friend had said. It was clear that Lady Symington was all too aware of the sort of gentleman her brother was and that brought Anne a little relief. She was able to speak freely with Lady Symington, she understood, and that was an excellent thing indeed.

"My brother has had a great deal of trouble with Henley," Lady Symington continued, seemingly quite willing to share her own thoughts with Anne. "Henley has often got himself into difficulty – by his own hand, you understand – and for whatever reason, has expected Denfield to chase after him and come to his aid."

A little surprised, Anne turned to look at Lady Symington a little better and saw her nodding as if to confirm it all.

"Denfield has gone, of course," Lady Symington said, in answer to Anne's silent question, "because he feels responsible for Henley as his younger brother, *and* because he feels responsibility to his family name. But he has given that all up now. He will not come to Henley's aid any longer, no matter what happens." A slight frown pulled at her forehead. "I tell you this in confidence, of course, for I believe that I can trust you."

"You can," Anne said quickly, speaking with more urgency than she had meant. "I am not going to breathe a word of this to anyone, not even to my aunt, if you would wish it."

"Oh, you may speak of it to Lady Mayhew if you wish," Lady Symington smiled. "I meant only that it is not to become gossip but being aware that you are entirely disinclined towards gossip, I am able to speak openly to you. I tell you of this also so that you might understand how foolish my brother is and the situation that you yourself are stepping into. Henley will always be an annoyance, I think, until he decides that he ought to change his ways. When that day will come, however, I do not know."

"I appreciate your honesty and your trust in me." Anne gave Lady Symington a quick smile. "I believe your brother – that is, Lord Denfield – to be a gentleman of excellent character. I am sure that whatever he decides as regards Lord Henley will be fair, both now and in the future."

Lady Symington's expression softened. "It seems as though you understand my brother more than I expected," came the quiet reply. "Lord Denfield is certainly a gentleman who knows exactly what is expected of him and he will do everything in his power to do it."

Anne said nothing in response, though she did nod. Instead, she turned her attention to the very gentleman in question who sat at the very head of the table, given that he was master of the house. He was laughing at something that had been said, something that Anne had missed completely, and the warmth in his expression, the way his blue eyes danced made her heart skip a beat. When his eyes turned to hers, as though he had somehow known that she had been looking at him, Anne's breath hitched as her face burned hot though she could not pull her eyes away. When she had first come to the idea of being wed to Lord Denfield, it had been something of a shock but now, now that she looked upon him and saw all that he was and all that he *could* be to her, she found her heart thrilled with the sheer joy of it all. What more could she ask for in a husband?

***

"I saw you speaking at length to Julia." Lord Denfield smiled as Anne nodded. "It seems as though she was quite right to insist on the seating arrangements though I would much have preferred to be sitting with you myself."

Anne blinked in surprise at his confession, looking up into his face and seeing the slight roundness of his eyes, perhaps betraying that he himself had not meant to speak so. "You would?"

Lord Denfield ducked his head but nodded. "Yes, of course. You are my betrothed, after all." Lifting his gaze, he looked at her again. "The banns will be called this Sunday. After that, we have two weeks – a fortnight – until we can marry. The time has come quickly, has it not?"

"It has." Anne smiled back at him, a little astonished at just how much she desired such a thing. To stand up in church and make her vows brought her a little anxiety, of course, but it also brought her a good deal of happiness at the thought. She would be secure then. Secure, kept safe, kept *back* from her father and instead, held tightly in the arms of Lord Denfield.

"The *ton* have not been gossiping about the match too much," Lord Denfield continued, speaking quietly so that the others in the drawing room would not overhear them. After dinner, the ladies had made their way through first with the gentlemen coming a short while thereafter. Everyone was now conversing, with Lady Symington playing the pianoforte and filling the room with a sweet ambience.

"No, they have not. That is a good thing." Anne smiled gently, keeping her gaze fixed to his and wondering just how many of the other guests were aware of their presence. She had been wandering around the room, taking everything in and giving herself a short respite from conversation when Lord Denfield had come to join her, pinning her between a bookcase and the wall behind her. It made for a very private conversation, especially with the dark shadows that pulled them back into themselves all the more. "I am grateful for your willingness to be so considerate in that regard."

Lord Denfield smiled back at her, though when his hand touched hers, when his fingers ran over hers and his thumb traced the back of her hand, fire began to erupt from her very core. Suddenly, there was no thought of what she could say back to him, no consideration of what was next to be said. Her breath was quickening, her heart beginning to pound as Lord Denfield took a small step closer, his voice lowering all the more. "I would consider and I would do anything, should it make you happy."

"Shall we dance?"

Anne jumped in surprise at the loud voice of Lord Symington which broke through the room. There was laughter and delight as some of the other dinner guests found themselves a partner and stepped to the floor – but Lord Denfield did not move.

Suddenly, Anne was very grateful for the bookcase which hid her from the guests' eyes, for the shadows which clung to Lord Denfield. She did not want to dance. She did not want to step out with even Lord Denfield himself, did not want to make her way forward and stand in line with everyone else. All she wanted was to linger here, to be in company with Lord Denfield so that this wondrous, overwhelming excitement might linger for just a little longer.

"Miss Jennings," Lord Denfield began, his voice a little louder than a whisper now, a whisper which ran like lightening across her skin. "I – "

"Would you not call me Anne?"

106

Lord Denfield paused, then smiled back at her. "If you should wish me to."

"When we are not in company, I can see no reason for us not to be a little less formal, can you?" Anne asked, both astonished at her own audacity and glad at the ease with which she spoke to this gentleman. There truly was a strong connection between them, was there not? A joy – a happiness – which she herself felt growing with every word that they shared. "But only if you wish it, I – "

"Of *course*, I wish it." Without warning, Lord Denfield grasped her hand and, inclining his head, lifted her hand to his lips and pressed a kiss to the back of it.

Anne went hot all over, barely able to move as he lingered there for a good deal longer than she had expected. When he lifted his head, there was a sharpness to his gaze that she had not seen before and a sweetness to his smile which had never been there before either. She could barely breathe, pressing one hand lightly to her stomach as he continued to grasp her hand, his eyes searching her face though quite what it was he was looking for, she did not know.

"Anne," he said, simply, the tenderness in his voice making her heart ache. "I do like your name."

"Truly?" Her own voice was hoarse, her face aflame as he smiled at her again.

"Truly," he said, softly, his nearness to her so close that there was barely an inch between them. "I like your name a great deal. Just as I like you."

"Miss Jennings? Should you like to dance?"

The moment was shattered as Lord Symington's voice filled the room, clearly searching for her.

"Alas, she cannot," Lord Denfield said quickly, stepping out and taking Anne with him, her hand now firmly caught in his. "For she has already agreed to dance with me."

The room was filled with smiles and tender murmurs and though Anne's face was still hot and embarrassed, she could not help but smile as Lord Denfield led her down to dance with his other guests in the center of the drawing room. Quite what would have happened had they not been interrupted, she did not know but all the same, the joy of the moment they *had* shared was enough to keep that smile pinned to her face for the rest of the evening.

Chapter Sixteen

Peter inclined his head as Lady Mayhew rose to her feet, bobbing a curtsy.

"If you are looking for Miss Jennings, I am afraid she has gone to town with Lady Grace and her mother," Lady Mayhew began, though she gestured for Peter to sit down. "I am sorry you have missed her."

"But it is you that I came to see," Peter told her, making Lady Mayhew's eyes widen. "There is something I wished to ask you."

"Oh?"

Taking a moment to prepare his words, Peter spread out his hands. "It is a sensitive matter and if you would prefer that I did not speak of it, I quite understand."

Lady Mayhew smiled. "Please, do feel free to speak as honestly as you wish about any subject. You have already proven your character so I do not feel any concern in that regard."

Peter put his hands back to his lap. "You are very kind. What I wish to speak of is Lady Ellon."

In that one instant, Lady Mayhew's smile faded and a glint came into her eyes.

"I would very much like her to be present for the wedding, if it were possible," Peter continued, quickly, seeing the sharpness fade from Lady Mayhew's eyes. "I have a letter here, already written, to inform her of what is taking place, the date and time of the wedding as well as the assurance that Lord Ellon will *not* be present. Might I ask you to send it to Lady Ellon on my behalf? Mayhap with a note to assure her that this is entirely genuine?"

"Oh, Lord Denfield." Lady Mayhew blinked rapidly, her eyes filled with tears which Peter had not at all expected. "You are *most* considerate."

"I know that Miss Jennings misses her mother a great deal, though she has explained a little as to why Lady Ellon remains where she is," Peter replied, gently. "I do not wish to press the lady, however. If you think it best that the letter is not sent, then –"

"No, no, I think it a marvelous idea!" Lady Mayhew exclaimed, rising at once to take the letter from him. "I have written to her only last week informing her of what has happened and I know she would be very glad to receive a letter from you yourself! I will, of course, add in a small note to confirm it all."

"The wedding is only a fortnight away so it must go at once," Peter said, slowly, seeing Lady Mayhew nod. "Will that be enough time? I am sorry I only thought of this recently."

"More than enough time," came the reply. "Have no fear, Lord Mayhew. You leave this all entirely to me."

Peter rose to his feet. "Thank you, Lady Mayhew. I shall not take up any more of your time."

"But of course." Smiling, she reached out one hand and Peter bowed over it. "I am very grateful to you for your consideration in all of this."

"I only want to make Miss Jennings as happy as she can be." Peter rose and stood tall. "Do excuse me, I must make my way into town. I have one or two errands which must be taken care of at once."

Lady Mayhew nodded. "Of course. Mayhap you will see Anne there for, as I have said, Lady Grace took them both for a short promenade around town."

"Then I must hope that I shall," Peter answered, making his way to the door. "Good afternoon, Lady Mayhew."

***

As Peter made his way from his solicitors, he could not help but notice the way his heart ached as he searched for Miss Jennings. The desire to see her, to be in her company once more and to see her smile was so great, so overwhelming that he could barely think of what it was that he had come to town to do. Yes, he had gone to see his solicitors but was there not something else that he intended?

Hearing two ladies laughing, he turned his head and, much to his delight, saw both Miss Jennings and Lady Grace emerging from the bookshop. His heart leapt and he hurried towards them both, seeing how Miss Jennings' smile grew as he came closer to her.

"Good afternoon, Lady Grace, Miss Jennings," he exclaimed, bowing quickly. "How wonderful to see you both here."

"We were just in the bookshop," Miss Jennings told him, quickly taking his arm as Lady Grace's mother stepped out from the bookshop also, nodding and smiling at him which he quickly returned. "Did you have business in town?"

"I did." Walking along with her, with Lady Grace on his other side, Peter continued on the conversation for some time, asking what it was that Lady Grace and Miss Jennings had purchased at the bookshop and finding himself very happy indeed to be in company with them both. He had quite forgotten what his other errand was to be though that did not seem to matter any longer. All that he desired was right here.

"Do excuse me for a moment." Lady Grace stepped back to speak to her mother, leaving Peter and Miss Jennings to talk together.

"Are you to attend Lord Crestwood's ball this evening?" Peter asked, smiling warmly when she nodded. "And will you save me the waltz?"

Miss Jennings' face flushed though she smiled back at him. "Of course. I should be glad to."

"Very good. I do very much enjoy dancing with you, Anne." The smile on his face grew all the more as her cheeks grew pink, delighted to see the happiness in her expression as she looked back at him.

"My lord?"

A voice interrupted his thoughts and, irritated, Peter turned his head to see none other than his brother's messenger standing there, though the man's head was bowed and his hands gripped tightly in front of him.

"Not now," he stated tightly, turning back to see Miss Jennings frowning, clearly uncertain as to who this man was and what he was doing. "Now is not the time for requests." Gesturing to him, Peter began to explain to Miss Jennings who he was. "My brother has sent this man to me – as he often does – in order to gain something from me. No doubt my brother has got himself into some sort of difficulty and though I have already stated that I will not continue to come to his aid in the way that he desires, he appears to be quite determined to continue to try me."

"I see." Miss Jennings turned to look at the messenger, who now had a look of confusion on his face, perhaps uncertain as to what it was he was meant to do. His irritation growing, Peter turned more fully towards the fellow, letting out a breath of exasperation as he gestured to him.

"You might as well tell me what it is that my brother has asked you to tell me so that I might give you a response and send you on your way," he said, seeing the man nodding. "What is it?"

The man harrumphed, then put his hands behind his back, ready to begin. "Lord Henley begs twenty pounds from you."

Peter's eyes flared, embarrassment beginning to climb up his spine. "I beg your pardon?"

The messenger shook his head. "I do not know what else to say, Lord Denfield. That is all that was asked of me."

"Twenty pounds?" Peter repeated, for though it was not a great deal considering how much he possessed by way of his fortune, it was a significant amount to ask for. "For what purpose, might I ask?"

This made the man drop his head forward, so that his chin almost rested on his chest. "Lord Henley is presently engaged in a card game, Lord Denfield."

Anger spiraled through Peter's chest. "Cards?"

"Yes, my lord."

"And no doubt, he has run out of funds."

The man nodded. "Yes, my lord."

Rubbing one hand over his eyes, Peter took a moment to make certain his tone was measured before he spoke again, eagerly attempting not to lose his temper in front of Miss Jennings. He did not want to appear overly harsh but his brother had to understand that this sort of thing would not be tolerated any longer. "I have already told my brother that he is not to expect any sort of aid from me when he gets himself into these difficult situations," he said slowly, making sure to choose each word carefully. "I am afraid I cannot – I will not – help him here."

The messenger did not hesitate but hurried away at once, leaving Peter with a heavy heart as he turned back to Miss Jennings. How he prayed she would understand his actions! How he hoped that she would not think him harsh or cruel!

"My brother is – "

"Julia... that is to say, Lady Symington, already explained this to me." Miss Jennings put her hand back to his arm, her lips curving gently. "Do not feel as though you have any requirement to explain, Lord Denfield. I quite understand."

"You do?" Relief poured into him and as she nodded, Peter's heart filled with a stronger affection for her than he had ever felt before. "You do not know how much I value and appreciate that, Miss Jennings. I am doing what I feel must be done while, at the same time, worrying about the consequences which will inevitably follow."

Her expression grew sympathetic. "It must be a heavy burden for you, Lord Denfield."

"It can be," he admitted, "though to know that you understand and that you accept the situation, such as it is, is a great relief to me."

That smile grew but before she could say anything more, Lady Grace returned to them and the conversation went in an entirely different direction. As they walked, however, Peter considered all that was in his heart and, in doing so, found himself smiling despite all that had just taken place with his brother's foolish request. Miss Jennings – Anne – was making a greater impression upon his heart than he had ever anticipated. There was nothing he could not share with her, nothing that he felt the need to keep back for fear that she would not understand. She was nothing but understanding and sympathy and for that, Peter found himself nothing short of grateful.

Chapter Seventeen

"Now, what do you think of it?"

Anne regarded herself in the full length mirror, taking in what was to be her wedding gown. It was made of heavy silk, the gentle green pulling the green into focus in her eyes and a severe amount of detailing and lace. "This is the most beautiful dress I think I have ever worn, Aunt."

"Which is just as it should be!" Lady Mayhew exclaimed, a laughing joy in her eyes. "After all, you are only married once, are you not? How wonderful a day that is to be."

Anne smiled and twirled gently, seeing her gown settling back into place, rustling softly as it did so. This truly was the most magnificent gown and she was utterly delighted with it.

Just as I am delighted with marrying Lord Denfield.

The smile which spread across her face was so wide and her joy so utterly complete, she could barely contain it. A lump rose in her throat, happy tears in her eyes as her aunt spoke quickly to the modiste, asking for a little more lace at the collar of Anne's dress. Silently, Anne composed herself but began to consider what it would be like to stand by Lord Denfield and to take his hand and promise herself to him. Would he be just as pleased as she to be wed?

"If you are worrying about what Lord Denfield will think, I can assure you that he will be overwhelmed by your beauty." Lady Mayhew turned back to her, as though somehow she had known what Anne had been thinking. "You do care for him, do you not?"

A deep heat began to rise in Anne's cheeks as she struggled to look her aunt in the eye. "I – I do feel something for him, I will admit that." Relieved that the modiste had stepped away for a few minutes, meaning that she was not to be overheard, Anne spread out her hands. "I do not know what it is, Aunt, but I am glad to be in his company."

"As well you should. Clearly, he is delighted to be in *your* company also, given the way that he was standing so *very* close to you at the dinner some evenings ago." A twinkle came into Lady Mayhew's eye as Anne's face flushed all the more. "Yes, I saw you standing together in what was very intimate conversation."

"I do hope you did not think me improper?" Anne asked, suddenly a little afraid that her aunt was upset with her. "I did not know what else to do and to be truthful, I did not want to step away from him."

"Of course you did not!" Lady Mayhew exclaimed, laughing. "My dear girl, I did not think you improper in the least! Though I must say, I am glad to know that you do feel something for Lord Denfield. He does appear to be an excellent gentleman and to see now that he cares for you in the way that you care for him does make my heart very happy indeed."

Anne swallowed hard. "You think that he cares for me?"

Lady Mayhew's smile grew tender. "I do not only think it, I know it," she answered, gently. "I saw it in the way that he stood so close to you, in the tenderness that shone in his eyes when you both danced together. Yes, my dear girl, that gentleman is half in love with you, if not quite lost in love already!"

The thought of that was so overwhelming, Anne did not know whether she wanted to laugh or cry such was the joy in her heart. The modiste returned, however, and the conversation was drawn to a close, leaving Anne to change into her old gown so that the wedding gown could be given its final alterations.

"The next time you step into this gown shall be your wedding day," Lady Mayhew said happily, linking arms with Anne as they made their way from the shop. "How wonderful a day that will be."

"Indeed it shall be, Aunt," Anne agreed, softly, her mind and heart filled only with thoughts of Lord Denfield as they waited for the carriage to be brought around. "And it is less than two weeks away!"

Lady Mayhew smiled and pressed her arm. "Lord Denfield cares for you," she said, quietly. "I have an absolute assurance about that and, when he comes to take you as his bride, I am certain that he shall do so with joy. You will love one another and have a long and happy marriage, I am sure of it."

Anne let herself smile as a gentle contentment rushed through her. The carriage came to a stop in front of her and Anne, without thinking or even so much as looking up, stepped forward, her aunt's arm falling away, before making to step inside.

"Well, I did not think it would be as easy as this to steal you away but it seems that fate has smiled upon me!"

"Anne!"

Anne did not know what was happening. The cry of her aunt, the cruel, harsh tone mingling with it, the shock of being wrenched into the carriage and the dull thud of the carriage door being shut behind her made her dizzy with confusion and she found herself slumped back on the seat as the carriage itself began to roll away. Blinking furiously, she stared into the eyes of Lord Henley, utterly confused as to what he was doing and the intention behind it.

The man chuckled darkly and folded his hands in his lap. "And here I was, thinking I would have to cajole you into the carriage, that I would have to lie terribly about Denfield in order to place you in here – and quite how I was to rid you of your aunt, I did not know. But I have been fortunate enough, it seems, to have you step inside without so much as a thought!"

"You… you wanted me to ride with you?" Anne's voice was hoarse, a barely-there whisper and she shrank back in horror as Lord Henley nodded, chuckling as he did so.

"Not only ride with me, Miss Jennings, but to be stolen away by me!" he laughed, his jaw tightening as his eyes flashed. "My stupid brother will be forced into action and I shall gain what I desire."

Fear wrapped a tight hold around Anne's heart and she took in short, slow breaths in a vain attempt to calm its suddenly frantic beating.

"You are aware, I am sure, that my brother has decided he will no longer come to my aid when I require it," Lord Henley continued, sniffing as though this kidnapping of her was just to be expected. "I have decided, therefore, that this is not to be borne. Consequently, I have taken you into my care in the hopes of changing my brother's mind."

Anne swallowed the ache in her throat, aware of the trembling which now took over her frame. "You… you intend to use me as leverage?"

"But of course." Lord Henley lifted his shoulders and let them fall. "Though it might be that my brother will refuse to marry you once he realises that you have been in company with me, entirely unchaperoned!" He laughed and the whole carriage filled with a dark shadow which, even though Anne squeezed her eyes

116

closed, did not dissipate. "I am a gentleman who cannot be trusted, who has darkness within him and who has nothing but cruelty where one's heart ought to be. I am sure that you understand, Miss Jennings, that there *is* a chance that my brother will not do as I expect but that was a risk that I was willing to take."

Having no response for this, Anne could do nothing but stare at him, her whole being frozen with a dreadful fear which would not release its hold. Rather, it gripped her all the harder, burning through to her very bones as Lord Henley merely smiled, as though she ought to be quite contented with all that was happening.

"We are not going far," he promised her, though that smile on his face spoke of a conniving which was going to pull her into his scheme no matter what she wanted. "But it will not be easy for my brother to find us."

"What... " Anne could barely get the question out, the fear in her heart stealing her very senses away. "What are you going to do?"

Lord Henley laughed and Anne closed her eyes, simply to shut out the sight of him. "Do? I will do nothing at present but write to my brother and inform him that I have you. I will, thereafter, demand that he pay the debts I have accumulated – debts which he refused to even *consider* when I sent my messenger to him! I do not like his change of mind in that regard. He is my brother after all, and I expect him to help me when I need it!"

Anne said nothing, recalling all that Lord Denfield had said about his brother, remembering how he had stated that he would not do anything to come to his assistance again, given all that he had done. She had understood his reasons and had agreed with it entirely – but clearly, Lord Henley was displeased by such a decision. Evidently, he expected his brother to do just as he was asked, regardless of what it was. And now that Lord Henley was not about to be given what he wanted, he was resorting to extreme measures to achieve it.

"Nothing will happen to you for the moment," Lord Henley finished, carelessly waving a hand as though Anne ought to be glad of such a mercy. "Though there is danger enough in being in the presence of a gentleman unchaperoned, is there not?" He laughed harshly as tears began to form behind Anne's eyes. "If the *ton* were to find out, then I do not know what would happen! Of course, there would be a good deal of gossip about you and whether or not my brother would still marry you... mayhap *I* should end up marrying you after all, Miss Jennings! What foolishness that would be."

Anne let out a sob and covered her face with her hands, barely hearing Lord Henley begin to berate her for her tears. This was a dreadful circumstance, one that she had not even imagined and yet here she was, sitting with Lord Henley and under great threat. Whatever was she to do?

Chapter Eighteen

"My lord?"

Peter looked up at the footman. "Yes?"

"Lady Mayhew – "

Before he could finish speaking, the lady in question rushed into the room, her face pale, her eyes wide and staring. "Lord Denfield?"

"Yes, Lady Mayhew." Peter rose to his feet at once, putting the quill back in the pot, concerned at the fright he saw on her face. "Whatever is the matter?"

"It is Anne!" she exclaimed, much to his surprise grasping his jacket with one hand, the other going to his arm. "He has taken her in his carriage!"

Peter frowned. "Who?"

"Your brother! Lord Henley!"

Staring at the lady, his heart and mind filled with confusion, Peter blinked rapidly, only for the door to open and the footman to announce Lord and Lady Symington had arrived and were now sitting in the drawing room, waiting for him. Swallowing hard, Peter gave the man a nod and then, with his breath wrapping tightly in his chest, turned to look again at Lady Mayhew. "I – I was to take tea with Julia and Symington," he said, hoarsely. "Might you join me? Whatever has happened ought to be told to them also."

The lady nodded, her tight grip slowly releasing as she stepped back, though Peter caught the tears in her eyes.

"A tea tray," he said tersely, as the footman nodded. "Please, Lady Mayhew, come this way." Walking with her, Peter kept her hand on his arm, a little concerned that she might be feeling faint or weak given what had happened. They walked in silence to the drawing room, though the smile Julia sent them both when they stepped inside quickly faded away.

"Whatever has happened?" she asked, hurrying towards them both and taking Lady Mayhew's arm instead of Peter. "Lady Mayhew, please do sit down. Is there tea coming, brother?"

Peter nodded but instead of sitting, went to pour a small measure of brandy into a glass for Lady Mayhew, which she accepted without a word. Peter returned to pour one for himself and one for Lord Symington, just as the tea trays were brought in. Waiting impatiently for the servants to leave, he gave Lady Mayhew a nod, silently asking her to repeat her story again.

"Lord Henley has taken Anne," Lady Mayhew explained, making Julia gasp in shock, as Lord Symington frowned heavily. "We were coming out of the modiste and a carriage drew up. We..." She closed her eyes, her breathing shuddering before taking another sip of her brandy. "We were waiting for my carriage and I am sure that Anne thought the carriage ours. She did not look up and, I believe, was deep in thought about the upcoming wedding, given that we had been at the modiste in preparation for her wedding day. I spoke too late, not realising what was happening until it was much too late."

Peter began to pace up and down the room, his heart heavy with both grief and frustration over his brother's actions. "And it was Henley in the carriage?"

"Yes." Lady Mayhew sniffed and pulling out a handkerchief, dabbed at her eyes. "He was clearly hoping that, somehow, he would pull Anne into the carriage and make off with her, though it must have been a good deal easier than he anticipated."

"But why would he do such a thing?" Julia asked, shock filling her voice and stealing the strength from it. "Why would he take Anne from you?"

"I do not know." Lady Mayhew's eyes closed again and she wiped them with her handkerchief. "I do not understand. I thought that he had apologised to her, that he had made it quite clear that what he had done, he was sorry for. Why, then, would he steal her away like this?"

All eyes turned to Peter but he could give no answer. His shoulders lifted and fell though he continued to pace, his feet

119

heavy on the carpet, his shoulders low and expression heavy. Whatever his brother was doing, Peter had no understanding of either his actions or his intentions, though his heart burned with a furious anger over what he had done.

Is Anne well? he wondered, suddenly a little afraid for her. *What if Henley does something foolish? What if he demeans her in some way?*

"She is without a chaperone," Lady Mayhew cried, her heart clearly breaking for her niece. "If the *ton* were to hear of this, then – "

"The *ton* will *not* hear of it." Peter continued to stride up and down the room, his expression set as he set his gaze to the floor rather than look at anyone. "None of the servants are present and so, they cannot whisper of it. And I am sure that none of us wish to say anything to anyone that might injure her further."

There came a few murmurs of agreement and Peter let out a slow breath, trying to dampen down his anger and, instead, replace it with calm thinking. It did not come easily.

"What about the servants at the house?" Lady Mayhew asked, her voice still thin and quiet. "They will notice that Anne is away from home – that she does not sleep in her own bed – and that will cause them to whisper, I am sure! I will do my utmost to keep them from speaking so, but I am sure we all know what servants can be like."

Peter scowled. No matter how firm a master or mistress might be, their servants could not be trusted. That was why he himself was determined to keep his staff away from this room *and* from the knowledge of Miss Jennings' disappearance.

"You must say that Miss Jennings decided to stay with me for the night – or even for two or three, if this goes on," Julia suggested, as Lady Mayhew turned watery eyes to her. "I will make a bedroom up and make it appear as though Miss Jennings has slept there."

"But what about breakfast? And the evening before?" Lord Symington asked, clearly not disagreeing with his wife's suggestion but pointing out a slight flaw in it. "The servants might very well step inside and realise that Miss Jennings is not in that room and has not slept in that bed."

"I have it," Peter interjected, looking again to Lady Mayhew.

"You may state that Miss Jennings is unwell and is unable to be entertained by friends of visitors. Keep her at your home rather than pretend she is at Julia's. Make a bundle of clothes in the bed and state that she is not to be disturbed."

Lady Mayhew nodded slowly. "I can do that. But that does not give me any hope about *finding* Anne."

"No, it does not," Peter admitted, quietly. "But I must hope that soon, something will occur – maybe even a recognition from Lord Henley that he cannot continue to behave in this manner – and thereafter, all will be well." He said this with more hope than he felt but doubt surely lingered in his expression.

"But that is no good!" Julia exclaimed, getting to her feet and putting her hands to her hips. "We must *do* something."

"What *can* we do?" Lord Symington asked, looking to his wife and spreading his hands. "There is nothing that we can do, save for sending someone to his house to see if he is present there, though I think that in itself is fruitless, given that he will certainly *not* be there."

Peter nodded. "I am inclined to agree," he said, quietly, gesturing to Julia. "Might you pour some tea for Lady Mayhew and yourself? That might be something with which we can begin, at least."

Julia nodded though Peter rang the bell, deciding to send someone to Lord Henley's townhouse in the faint hope that he might have been foolish enough to have returned there already. A knock came to the door almost at once and, a little surprised at the speed of the servant's answer, Peter called for the footman to come in, only for the butler to appear with a silver tray in his hand. And upon the silver tray was a note.

"My lord." The butler inclined his head and Peter took it, looking down and seeing the sign pressed into the wax, his heart thudding furiously as he took in his brother's seal.

"It is from Henley." Dismissing the butler, he waited for a few moments after the door closed before he broke the seal and opened the note, determined not to be overheard. Reading it quickly, he let out a slow breath and then, lifting his eyes to the waiting company, he began to speak it aloud.

"As I have said, this is from Henley," he began. "It reads as follows. *'Brother, I am sure that by now, you will have heard that I* have Miss Jennings in my company – and what a fine creature she is! I am most despondent, however, that you have decided not to respond to my urgent requests for help these last few weeks and therefore, I have taken it upon myself to separate you from Miss Jennings.'"

"Separate?" Julia repeated, her eyes wide and her face rather pale. "For what purpose?"

With a nod, Peter continued to read. "'I do not think that it is fair of you to pull back from me in the way that you have. I have found it deeply distressing to send my messenger to you in request for your help, only to be told that you will not either be coming to my aid or sending me the money I require to remove myself from a particularly difficult situation. Therefore, I think that a change is required.'"

"So he is blackmailing you," Lord Symington interrupted, as Lady Mayhew sipped her tea, her face like parchment, both hands gripping the cup rather than holding it delicately as was proper. "What does he demand?"

Peter cleared his throat, tension rippling up his spine. "'I ask you now not for twenty pounds, as I requested some days ago, but fifty pounds to prove to me that you will do as I ask. Once that is done, I will consider what must happen next.'"

Silence filled the room.

"There is one final part," Peter finished, his throat constricting. "''Miss Jennings will stay with me until I have decided what you must do in order to prove yourself to be the loyal, dependable brother I have come to know. I should not like society to know of her presence here with me, of course, but if you do not do as I require, then I am afraid that I may have to let it be known that she is with me and entirely unchaperoned. What then, brother? Will you turn from her? Will I be forced to take her as my bride instead? I confess that I have no desire to wed the lady, though mayhap her dowry would be a little useful. I shall give you an hour to fetch the money and will send another note to tell you where to bring it. Do not fail me, brother. Do not fail Miss Jennings.'"

Peter handed the note to Lord Symington to read for himself before coming to sit down by Julia, sinking down beside her, putting his elbows on his knees and burying his fingers into his hair as he dropped his head. His mind was whirring, horror streaking through him as he tried to find a way to work through what his brother had demanded of him.

"This is all my fault."

"No, it is not!" Julia exclaimed at once, putting her hand to his shoulder. "This is Henley's wicked mind. It is nothing to do with you!"

"Yes, it is." Looking up at her, Peter felt the guilt tear at his heart. "If I had not stepped back from helping Henley, if I had not told him that I would *not* do anything more to help him, then he would never have been driven to this desperation. He would have continued on in his foolish ways and while I would have been irritated and frustrated at the interruption, I would have been able to contend with it." Swallowing hard, he looked to Lady Mayhew. "Lady Mayhew, I am sorry for my part in this."

Lady Mayhew studied him for a moment, then shook her head. "I agree with your sister that this is not your doing," she said, quietly. "Anne spoke to me about this. She told me of your decision as regards your brother and I quite agree with you that it was the right – and the fair thing – to do. This is not your fault and certainly, I do not hold anything against you in that regard. What we must decide now, however, is what is to be done!"

The guilt which clung to Peter was relentless, however, and though he understood what was being said, though he agreed that there was reason and purpose behind what he had done as regarded his brother, he could not help but feel responsible. "I will *not* turn from her, Lady Mayhew. I want you to understand that, to trust my word when I tell you that no matter what happens, I will never turn my back on the lady. I have come to care for Miss Jennings a great deal and I confess that to you willingly, so that you might be convinced of my regard for her."

Despite the tension in her expression, despite the fear which lingered in her eyes, Peter saw the way her lips curved gently, reassuring him.

"I quite believe that, Lord Denfield," Lady Mayhew said, quietly. "I have no doubt in my mind that my niece's future is quite safe with you."

"It is."

Lord Symington cleared his throat. "Will you give your

brother the fifty pounds?"

"Of course I shall!"

"Knowing that he will continue to make demand after demand of you," Lord Symington continued, his eyebrow lifting just a little. "I am not saying that you ought not to do so, of course, for Miss Jennings' safety must be guaranteed, only that there must be a plan that comes *with* that decision. We must find a way to stop your brother as well as secure Miss Jennings."

Feeling a little helpless, Peter looked back at his brother in law. "What is it that you would suggest?"

Lord Symington took a breath and then, after a moment, shook his head. "I do not know as yet but, if you are to send the money, then let us think and consider things together so that, once the letter from your brother arrives, telling you what is to be done, we already have a plan formed."

Considering this, Peter nodded slowly and then let out another sigh. "It is such a great shock, I cannot imagine what it is Miss Jennings is feeling at present."

Lady Mayhew's lips flattened. "She has a greater strength, a greater confidence within her than she believes," she said, with more determination than Peter had expected. "I have no doubt, that even if she is afraid, she too will be thinking and planning what can be done and how she can make her escape."

"Mayhap she will succeed," Peter replied, quietly. "My only prayer, however, is that if she does, she will not only be successful but that she will also make her way back to us in safety. I cannot wait for the moment when I will be able to hold her tight in my arms again."

Chapter Nineteen

Anne looked around the room and, rising to her feet, attempted to push the weakness out from within herself by walking around it. It was very sparsely decorated, with only a table, chair and sofa. There were windows looking outside but though she had already glanced outside, she had been able to see nothing of importance. There were no houses on the other side of the street, no company passing by. It must, Anne considered, be on the very edge of London. There was nothing that she recognized, nothing that she could see that brought even a hint of familiarity.

Sighing to herself, Anne looked out of the window again, taking in the sunshine which seemed to beckon to her, to call her back outside though she knew she could not escape from the room she was in at present. Lord Henley had brought her inside without a word, pushing open the door which, to Anne's confusion, had been open and unlocked. If this was not his townhouse, then were was it? She had tried to ask him, had tried to find the words to demand an answer from him but Lord Henley's hand had tightened around her arm as he had angrily told her to remain silent. No questions were to be asked and, even if they were, no answers would be given. Without another word, he had pushed her into this small room and, leaving it, had locked it behind him. Anne had tried to open it, had searched for another key hidden somewhere within the room itself but had eventually been forced to give up.

The tears had come, then. She had not held herself back, had not forced herself to keep the sadness and the tension inside. Her handkerchief had been quite damp by the time she had stopped shaking and though she did feel a little less strain, there was still a good deal of fear clinging to her.

The sound of a key scraping in the lock had her starting in fear and, with hasty feet, she hurried to sit on the sofa, making it just in time as the door opened and Lord Henley entered.

"I do not want you to become weak and faint," he said crisply, making it quite clear that the reason he had set down the tray with some food upon it, followed by a tea tray, was only for *his* benefit rather than her own. "I should not like to have to revive you. So eat. Drink."

He sat down next to her and Anne's skin crawled. Daring a glance, she saw his lifted eyebrows, saw him waiting for her to do as he had said. "I – I am not thirsty."

"But I insist."

Seeing that she was to have no other choice, Anne poured herself a cup of tea, added a little milk and then brought it to her lips. Despite the fact that she had told him she was not thirsty, the tea was marvelously refreshing.

"Eat."

Seeing there was no point in arguing, Anne picked up a honey cake and dutifully ate it, though it did not taste of sweetness but rather, it felt as though ash was in her mouth. Swallowing it, she sipped her tea again and watched Lord Henley rise to his feet, a calculated look in his eyes.

"Very good. I expect you to have eaten a little more and have drunk that pot of tea by the time I return."

"Return?" Anne could not help the word that slipped from her mouth and Lord Henley, who had pushed himself up out of the chair, froze and then slowly, sat back down. The tension Anne felt in her heart tightened all the more and, blinking furiously, she turned her head away so that she could not even see him.

"You are, I suppose, wondering what it is that you are doing here and what my intentions are," Lord Henley said, slowly though his voice was cold, his words clipped. "I have already told you, I intend to use your presence here to make certain my brother does what I want him to do. Now, I have written to him and expect his response very soon."

Anne did not see him but rather heard him rise fully from his chair, his footsteps making their way to the door rather than drawing closer to her.

"I am sure that my brother will have done what I have asked of him," came his voice, forcing Anne to turn her head to glance at him, hearing the smile in his voice and not understanding where it came from. "He cares far too much for you, Miss Jennings. He cares so much that it is utterly foolish, utterly ridiculous and, to my mind, utterly repulsive."

He put one hand on the door handle, ready to pull it open and step out and, in that one moment, an idea came so quickly into Anne's mind, she found herself speaking without thought.

126

"Why is it repulsive?"

Lord Henley blinked and though Anne trembled inwardly at the darkness in his expression and the anger in his eyes, she did not flinch but held his gaze with as much firmness as she dared, silently praying that what she hoped for would come to pass.

Lord Henley turned back towards her though one hand still lingered on the door handle, pulling the door open but not stepping out through it. "It is repulsive, Miss Jennings, because my brother has turned away from family and his responsibilities. Instead of doing what he has always done, instead of coming to my aid to help me whenever I ask him, he has decided to stop doing such a thing and remain at home! I have been waiting for his help, finding myself in difficult situations and expecting him to appear so that I might find relief and hope, but instead, there is nothing! My messenger returns with a note or a message to say that he will no longer come to help me, that he will not even send funds when I require them! And that is solely because of *your* presence, Miss Jennings. He has no thought of family any more but instead has thoughts only about you and the future you shall share together."

A knot tied itself in Anne's throat but she forced the words out anyway. "You cannot expect Lord Denfield to change and return to how he once was because of this, Lord Henley. Even if you ruin me, even if he steps away from me, can you truly believe that he will go back to the way he used to be?"

Lord Henley shrugged. "One way or the other, he will do as I ask, Miss Jennings. And if he permits you to be ruined, if he is contented to step back from you, then I *shall* hope that he will return to family and his previous way of life." Growing louder as he spoke, Lord Henley began to gesticulate with his free hand. "And if he *does* continue on with this fanciful connection to you, then regardless, he *will* return to how he once was with me! I shall have the help from my brother *and* the coin that I expect!"

Without another word, he turned and pulled the door tight shut behind him. It was a loud slam and made Anne jump with fright, though she stared at the door, her heart pounding in her chest as she prayed he would forget to lock it behind him, such was his fury. It was the idea which had come to her, the hope which now burned in her and as she stared at it, as she waited to hear the scrape of the key in the lock, all that met her was silence.

Closing her eyes, Anne let out a long, slow breath, hardly able to believe that what she had hoped for had succeeded. Lord Henley's anger had burned through him, had frightened her, yes, but had prompted him to storm out of the room, to leave her behind and to *forget* to lock the door.

She could make her escape.

Blinking rapidly, Anne rose from her chair and, on tiptoe for fear that Lord Henley would realize what he had done and would return. She dared not go near the door now, did not think that she could rush away from the house for fear that he was still present and would see her – and besides which, she did not know who else was in the house.

Looking out of the window, she watched for some minutes until, much to her relief, Lord Henley emerged from the house and walked down the street without so much as a glance behind him. She shrank back for fear that he would turn to look at her again but, after a few moments, saw him hail a hackney and, stepping inside, made his way around the corner.

Closing her eyes, Anne tried not to let the tears of relief which pressed behind her eyes escape, curling her hands into fists as she forced herself to take in long, slow breaths to steady herself. She had no knowledge as to where she was, had no coin by which to pay for a hackney or a carriage and did not know whether or not she was alone in this house and could, in fact, make her escape from it.

"But I am determined."

Opening her eyes, Anne lifted her chin and tried to encourage herself with silent whispers, telling herself that since she had already managed to manipulate Lord Henley into leaving the door unlocked, she could also find a way to make her escape. Somehow, she would find her way back to Lord Denfield... though quite whether her reputation would be intact, she could not say.

I must hope that he will accept me still, regardless, she thought to herself, slowly making her way to the door on silent feet, still afraid that there was someone else in the house. *I must hope that all Lord Henley said of him and his affection for me is true... for what else do I have to cling to except him?*

Chapter Twenty

"You have the money?"

"Of course I do." Peter scowled and ran one hand through his hair. "Though there is not yet another note from him to tell me where I am to take it."

"Yes, there is."

Peter turned at once, seeing Julia hurrying into the drawing room with Lady Mayhew only a little behind her.

"A man delivered this only a few minutes ago, though the butler said he ran from the door the moment it was delivered."

"No doubt paid well to do so." Irritated, Peter took the letter from his sister and broke the seal. Opening it, he read it aloud. "*'Take the money to the Bird Cage Walk in St James' Park at three o'clock. There, you shall see a gentleman standing with an empty bird cage in his hand. Ask him no questions but place the money in the bird cage and then return to your carriage. Once you have returned home, another message will be sent.'*"

"Oh, it is truly dreadful to think that our brother has concocted these dreadful things!" Julia pulled out her handkerchief, just as her husband came into the room, one arm going around his wife's shoulders as he sent an enquiring look towards Peter. Handing Lord Symington the letter, Peter drew in a deep breath. "I have no doubt that the gentleman with the empty bird cage in his hand will be one of our brother's acquaintances."

"Who I shall follow, of course." Lord Symington looked down at his wife. "You will remain at home, Julia."

"I most certainly shall not!" Julia's chin lifted, the tears in her eyes sparkling with indignation. "I am not about to step aside and wait for my brother and you to take action! No, I shall walk with my friend Lady Grace and – "

"Why do not you and I walk together, Lady Julia?" Lady Mayhew stepped closer, putting an end to Peter's intention that both the ladies would remain at home together. "Yes, your husband is to follow this gentleman – whoever he is – and Lord Denfield will have to return home for I have no doubt that he himself will be watched, to make sure that he does as is asked, but we have no reason to hide ourselves away! We could walk from the opposite direction, though we should have to leave almost at once."

Julia nodded eagerly, though Peter shared a despairing look with Lord Symington – his brother in law only shrugged.

"Yes, you and I could walk from one end of the park while you, brother, walk in from the other side!" Julia exclaimed, as Lady Mayhew turned her gaze towards him, clearly expecting him to agree. "I have every expectation that Henley will be expecting some of us but he surely cannot have brought many of his friends into this plan? There will only be one or two or maybe, at the very most, three and that means they cannot keep an eye upon all of us!"

"It would help, I suppose," Lord Symington agreed, slowly. "It would mean that they might be able to spy whoever is pursuing *you*, Denfield. It might even be your very own brother, watching you to make sure that you return to your carriage and, thereafter, to your townhouse. As he has said, he will not send another letter to you until you are safely back at home, which must mean he will be watching you in some way."

Seeing that there was sense in all that had been said, Peter nodded his agreement. "Very well. Then might I suggest, Julia, that Lady Mayhew and you depart almost at once. I must linger for another fifteen minutes or so before I make my departure, just so that I can be there on time. But please," he finished, reaching to catch Julia's hand before she stepped away, "do be careful. If there is even the smallest hint of darkness pursuing you, return home at once."

"We shall, Lord Denfield," Lady Mayhew promised, solemnly. "I shall watch Lady Symington as though she were my very own."

Peter released Julia's hand, thanked Lady Mayhew and watched as the two made their way from the room, his heart sinking lower and lower as the door closed behind them. The shame he felt in knowing that his brother had done such wickedness was almost overpowering, cowing him, pushing him low as he hung his head, the letter still in his hand.

"We shall overcome this." Lord Symington put one hand to Peter's shoulder, clearly aware of what he was feeling. "You will succeed, Denfield. One way or another, you will have Miss Jennings back safely."

"Though at what cost?" Peter asked, the question unanswered as Lord Symington shook his head, unable to say anything in response. "Just how far is my brother willing to go before he finally gives my dear Anne back into my arms?"

***

The Bird Cage Walk was so called because of the merry monarch, James I's, delight in the many aviaries which he had placed along the park edge. There were no such aviaries any longer though, at times, gentlemen and ladies did bring little birds in cages to show off to others. Therefore, Peter concluded, it would not be particularly unusual for a gentleman to be standing with an empty bird cage in one hand though, thus far, he had not seen anyone of that description.

Biting his lip, he continued to make his way slowly along the path, nodding to an acquaintance here and there but otherwise, keeping his gaze and his intentions fixed to the persons standing on either side. Some were speaking to others, some were clearly waiting for acquaintances or sweethearts to appear but none had a bird cage in their hand.

His breathing quickened as fright took a hold of him. What if his brother had lied? What if there was no gentleman here, no-one holding a bird cage, no-one watching for his return? What if this was all some sort of elaborate ploy by which his brother had an even darker intention?

There!

His eyes flared as he caught sight of a tall, thin gentleman who had a small bird cage in one hand. Taking him in, Peter considered whether he knew this man or not, considering the profile and the cut of the man's clothes but realizing that he did not, stepped closer, ready to do all that his brother had requested.

"I think you are expecting me." Seeing the thin man turn towards him, Peter pulled out the sealed letter from his pocket, a letter which not only begged his brother to release Miss Jennings but also contained the fifty pounds which had been requested. "And I am to place it in here, am I not?"

The gentleman said nothing. He did nothing other than to lift the cage with one hand and hold it open for Peter's letter. Placing

132

it inside, Peter lifted his gaze back to the gentleman's inscrutable expression, waiting for him to say something – but the gentleman did not. Instead, he merely closed the cage door, turned on his heel and walked away.

The urge to pursue him was so strong, Peter found himself taking a few steps closer, only to drop his head and let out a heavy sigh. *I cannot.*

The only thing he had to do now was turn around and return to his carriage and, thereafter, back to his townhouse. He had nothing more to do, nothing that he *could* do in order to help Miss Jennings. He had to trust that Lord Symington would be able to follow the gentleman with the bird cage, that maybe even Julia and Lady Mayhew would be able to find something else also.

He had done his part.

***

Stepping into his townhouse, the weight on Peter's heart grew all the more. With a long breath, he handed the butler his hat and his gloves but then found himself quite lost as to where he ought to go or what he ought to do. The hopelessness, the desperation that he felt was so strong, it was crippling. His chest tightened, his breathing coming in short, sharp gasps as he fought against the fear which burned right through him. What had he done in giving his brother what he wanted? Yes, they had come up with a plan where Lord Symington was going to follow after this gentleman and with his sister and Lady Mayhew walking through the park also, but what if they found nothing? What if the gentleman took a carriage and Lord Symington could not follow after him? Would Miss Jennings remain in further danger? It would not be long until the evening and what dark deeds would Henley have planned for her in that evening? Was she tied up? Injured? Broken? Closing his eyes tight, Peter took in a deep breath and dropped his head forward. How much he wanted to go out and search through London for Miss Jennings! How much he would give to make certain that she was safe!

I love her.

The thought came to him quickly and Peter's eyes flared, his heart tumbling as he blinked, taking in what he had thought, what he now felt and realizing the strength of it, the significance of it. This was more than just a gentle affection, a fleeting interest in the lady. This was a heart-rending love, something that burned through every part of him and made him realize that the only thing he wanted, the only thing he desired was to have Miss Jennings safe again in his arms.

"I want to tell her that I love her," he whispered to himself, making his way back to the drawing room, his heart beating quickly, his blood thundering in his veins as he stepped into the room, closed the door behind him and walking to the window. Looking out, his breath fogging the window, he imagined the moment he would have the lady back in his arms, back when he could look into her eyes and tell her the truth of his heart.

Could he hope that there would come a time when that could happen? Or was Miss Jennings lost to him forever?

Chapter Twenty-One

Anne tiptoed up the hallway, her heart beating so hard, it was the only thing she could hear. Every tiny sound made her jump, her skin prickling with fright but thus far, she seemed to be entirely alone in the house. She had considered making her way to the front door and to go out that way but her fear of Lord Henley returning had forced her to reconsider. Thus, she was now in search of the servants staircase, hoping beyond hope that the house would have no servants within it and that she, consequently, would be able to remove herself from the house without any difficulty.

Though quite what she was to do and where she was to go thereafter, Anne did not know. At least she still had her bonnet, her gloves and her spencer, meaning that she would appear quite commonplace – though a lady walking alone might catch the attention of some, depending on which part of London she was in.

And if I am in a part of London I do not recognise, then what shall I do?

Anne trembled and tried not to let her thoughts run away with her fear. The first thing she had to do was remove herself from this house and thereafter, she might worry as to what she ought to do. With relief, she spied the servants staircase and, on nimble feet, hurried towards it.

The sound of a key in the lock echoed towards her, which was swiftly followed by the door itself opening. Anne's whole body went cold but she did not hesitate, hurrying down the staircase and into the darker, shadowy rooms of the servants. She had no doubt that Lord Henley had returned, that he had come back from whatever it was he had gone to do and would soon find her missing. Her panic began to grow as she tried to find the door which would lead her outside, only for another thought to give her pause.

If she escaped from the house, would not Lord Henley see her? Would he not spy her rushing from him? What then was she to do?

A loud shout caught her ears and she pushed open the door that led outside without hesitation, desperate to remove herself from the prison where Lord Henley had thought to keep her. The air was fresh and sweet but she did not even notice it, hurrying to one end of the path and looking this way and that for fear that she would be discovered.

Surely he will not snatch me from the street?

Swallowing hard, Anne took in a deep breath and, steeling herself, hurried up the path and around the side of the house that led to the street. She stayed back a little, hiding herself from view should Lord Henley look out of the window. Her heart clamored, her fear pushing her to do more, to act, somehow, and yet she remained where she was, frozen in indecision.

A hackney came into view.

It was her only escape, her one chance to make her way to freedom, to go back to where Lord Denfield and safety lay. She had no coin, yes, but surely she could do something – say anything – to force the driver to do as she asked?

"Wait!"

Crying out, she hurried forward, stumbling a little as fear and hope drove her forward. She did not so much as pause as she came to the road itself, stepping out and only giving a brief glance to see if any other hackney or carriage was coming in the opposite direction. The hackney driver did not appear to see her or hear her given that he did not slow for even a moment, his hands holding the reins, his gaze away from her.

"Wait, please!" Hearing another shout, Anne looked over her shoulder, fearing that Lord Henley would have seen her before turning back to the hackney. Whether or not the driver had seen her, whether or not he had space for her, she did not care. Her only choice was to get inside and, pulling the door open – and even with the wheels still turning – she somehow forced herself inside.

"Good gracious!"

The voice of the occupant within the hackney was filled with surprise as Anne, breathing heavily, sat back opposite the lady and gentleman. She blinked, uncertain as to what to say, fearful that they were from the *ton,* only to notice the slightly dulled fabric of the lady's gown and the touch of wear to the gentleman's hat.

Perhaps she was safe enough.

"Pray forgive me," she said, hoarsely, as two sets of eyes stared back at her in utter astonishment. "I did not mean to startle you."

"You have climbed into our hackney – which we have already *paid* for, might I add – and seated yourself opposite us without even a word of explanation!" the gentleman exclaimed, as the lady Anne presumed to be his wife, nodded fervently though her lips quirked just a little, betraying, perhaps, a gentle hint of mirth.

"I am aware I have done so." Anne glanced over her shoulder, looking out of the window but of Lord Henley, there was no sign. "I must, of course, beg your forgiveness. I had no intention of doing any such thing but I am afraid I had no other choice."

"And why is that?"

The question from the lady left Anne silent for some moments. What was it she was meant to say by way of answer? Could she tell her the truth? If they were not from the *ton*, if they were not from high society, then could she trust them with that? Her heart told her no, she ought not to say a single thing to either of them for fear that their connections would bring her low. They might not be from high society but that was not to say that their brothers, sisters or friends were not.

"Are you going to answer?" the gentleman exclaimed, though the lady quickly put one hand over his, quietening him. Anne searched her face for a moment, hoping that what she saw there was sympathy rather than judgement as she sought her mind for an answer.

"As I have said, I am truly sorry for my actions," she began, speaking slowly so she might give great consideration to every word. "It must have been most unexpected for you both and not at all proper, I know. However, I would not have done so had it not been urgent."

"Urgent?" The lady's eyes flared. "You had an urgent desire to climb into our hackney?"

"I had a strong desire to get to a specific place in London," Anne explained, choosing not to say that she had thought to make an escape from a gentleman who had kept her captive for some time. "It is of the greatest urgency, otherwise I would not have done such a thing."

The gentleman and the lady exchanged a glance, looking to one another as though to enquire silently as to whether or not they believed Anne, though Anne herself remained silent. Her hands clasped tight together for, even if they let her stay in the hackney at this very moment, her problems would remain. She would not know where she was, how she was to get to either her aunt or Lord Denfield and certainly could not be sure as to whether or not Lord Henley would discover her within that time.

"I see." The gentleman sniffed, sounding a little less than pleased over what Anne had just disclosed. "I am very surprised indeed to think that a lady of your quality would, not only, be travelling unchaperoned but would also be without a carriage!"

Anne spread out her hands, heat rising into her cheeks. "I will admit that such a circumstance is very astonishing indeed, though as I have said, it does come with the greatest urgency. It is not a circumstance that I expected nor, in fact, that I had any control over."

Something seemed to ignite in the lady's eyes as Anne looked at her, as though she understood that there was some true difficulty in all that Anne had endured, that there was a genuineness in what Anne had expressed.

"Very well." The lady smiled quickly. "Tell us where we might place you so that you might go there at once."

Anne opened her mouth to speak, only for the gentleman to grip his wife's hand, his brows furrowing.

"My dear, I really must protest. We do not – "

"Do be quiet, Simmons." The lady spoke with a slight sharpness to her voice, her eyes searching her husband's face. "What if it was one of our daughters who found themselves in a difficult circumstance? Would you not want them to be shown kindness?"

"But we do not know if she speaks the truth!"

"I am no threat to you, I assure you," Anne said, quickly, her worry beginning to ease given the kindness of the lady. "I have nothing I can offer you by way of payment but I am well able to *repay* it, once I have returned."

The gentleman considered this though his wife nodded and smiled.

"You are very good to worry about such things but I will not have it," she said, reaching out and patting Anne's hand gently. "I can see there is worry in your eyes and whatever it is that troubles you, I will not further your concern by demanding that you repay us. No, it will be no trouble. Please, tell us where we are to take you and the driver will have you there in a moment."

With relief, Anne swallowed her tears which had quickly formed and, offering her grateful thanks, considered where she would be best to go. Would Lord Denfield be at home? Or would he be with her aunt? Deciding on the former, she gave them the address for Lord Denfield and, within a few minutes, the hackney driver had been informed of his new route and they were safely on their way.

Anne could not help the tears then. She was safe, it seemed, from Lord Henley's clutches and would soon be back with her aunt and her betrothed. The kindness of strangers – despite the gentleman's uncertainty – had relieved her of all her worry and anxiety and within a few minutes, she would surely be safe again.

"I am sorry for whatever it is that has troubled you so," the lady murmured, looking at Anne with concern in her expression as Anne pulled out her handkerchief and dabbed at her eyes. "It is clear to me that you have endured a great deal."

"I... I have, though it came at me entirely unexpectedly," Anne admitted, making sure not to say anything specific for fear that they might know Lord Henley and would spread news of her situation throughout London. Somehow, she had managed to escape from him with her reputation intact and did not want to ruin it now. "Though your kindness and generosity have saved me from a great deal more difficulty so pray do accept my gratitude once more."

The lady frowned and exchanged a look with her husband, who merely shrugged, clearly aware of what it was his wife was thinking even though she herself did not say a single word aloud. With a small nod, the lady looked back at Anne and then offered her a warm smile.

"We will not say anything of this to anyone, I can assure you. We are not as high in society as you, I dare say, but I am still very aware of the difficulties that gossip can bring. Let that not be another worry upon your mind. We will not ask your name nor seek out the owner of the house you step into. I hope that will bring you a little relief, my dear."

Anne dabbed at her eyes again, nodding and saying nothing,

given the tightness in her throat. She could not even find the strength to say thank you, could not tell them how grateful she was to them for their willingness to abstain from gossip. When the carriage drew up to the house, Anne swallowed her tears, pushed her handkerchief back into her pocket and looked at her two saviors, one after the other.

"I do not think I can express my gratitude," she whispered, her voice still filled with overwhelming emotion. "I thank you both, from the bottom of my heart."

The lady smiled, the gentleman barely nodded and Anne, after only a moment longer, pushed open the door of the hackney and stepped out onto the street. Without looking back, without hesitating, she climbed the stone steps and rapped on the front door which was opened after only a few moments.

"Miss Jennings!" The butler's face was one of astonishment as Anne stepped inside, suddenly weak with relief and fatigue. "Oh, my dear lady, do come in. Please, let me take your bonnet and your gloves. You there, go to fetch Lord Denfield at once!"

Seeing the maid scurrying away, Anne undid the ribbons of her bonnet as the butler shut the door behind her. She had only just handed the butler her bonnet and gloves when the sound of running feet met her ears and, as she lifted her head, found herself caught up in Lord Denfield's strong arms.

Chapter Twenty-Two

"My lord?"

Peter glanced at the maid, his fingers running over his chin as he fought for clarity, for even a moment of peace.

"Miss Jennings is here."

It took Peter a moment to comprehend what was being said to him. The maid held his gaze for a brief moment and then looked away, leaving him to stare at her as the understanding of what she had said finally made sense. Without a moment of hesitation, he ran to the door, flinging it open and hurrying out into the hallway.

The sight of her standing there, handing her gloves to the butler as though she had just come for an afternoon visit, gave him pause – but only for a moment. His feet propelled him forward, his heart pounding as he raced towards her. She turned to him, her eyes widening and then he caught her up in his arms, hardly daring to breathe as he held her tight against him.

"Anne," he whispered, his voice muffled against her shoulder. "Anne, you are safe."

She let out a choked sob, her arms tight around his neck, her feet off the floor as he held her all the more tightly. He could not say anything else, could not even *think*. All he could do was hold her close.

"Oh, Denfield." Miss Jennings sniffed and slowly, Peter put her down, fully aware that he had made an overly affectionate gesture in front of his staff but caring very little. After all, she was to be his wife very soon and he did not care whether or not his staff realized how much he cared for her.

"I was so very afraid," she whispered, her eyes shimmering with tears as he cupped her cheek, searching her face. "But I did what I could to escape from your brother. I only hope you have not been forced into something truly untoward?"

"Not in the least," he promised, squeezing her hand gently. "Come now, you must be exhausted." Looking to the butler, he gave him a nod. "Refreshments to be brought to the drawing room at once. Lady Symington and Lady Mayhew will return very soon, I hope, as will Lord Symington so you may prepare for them also."

The butler nodded and stepped away, leaving Peter to lead

Miss Jennings back to the drawing room, though he slipped one arm around her waist as they walked in order to both support her but also to keep himself close to her.

"I will hear all that you have to tell me but only once you are rested," he murmured, gently. "You are not to tire yourself out any more."

"I am not unwell, just a little weary."

Peter guided her into the room, setting her down onto the couch and quickly coming to sit beside her. "I am not at all surprised you are weary." His heart was still pounding furiously, his eyes taking her in, hardly able to believe that she was with him but yet, as he ran his thumb over the back of her hand, he slowly began to feel a sense of calm. His brother had no hold over him now. There was nothing that he could do any longer to attack Miss Jennings, nothing that he could threaten Peter with any longer. Miss Jennings was safe. She was here with him and she was *safe.*

"You were worried for me." Miss Jennings looked up at him, her eyes melding to his.

"I was. Of course I was!" Peter leaned a little closer, his other hand reaching out to touch her cheek. "You are so very dear to me, Anne. I confess that I have looked into my heart and realised just how much affection I have for you."

A tiny smile flicked up the corners of her mouth. "Truly?"

"Truly," he promised, his hand going to the nape of her neck, aware of the growing desire to bring his lips to hers but fearing that now was not the right moment for it. She had already endured so much. He ought not to be pushing himself forward any more. "We can talk of this later but – "

Before he could finish, Miss Jennings leaned closer and, before Peter knew what was happening or how he ought to respond, her mouth was on his and they were sharing a kiss. A swell of desire ran right through him, one arm going around her shoulders, pulling her closer, hearing the gentle sigh escaping from her as he broke the kiss for only a moment. He let himself kiss her again, turning his head just a little so it might deepen.

And then the sound of approaching voices forced them apart.

"Anne?"

The door flew open and Lady Mayhew rushed in, hurrying

towards Anne, her eyes wide.

"Anne! You are quite all right?"

"I am well, Aunt." Miss Jennings made to rise to her feet but her aunt enveloped her in a hug all the same. Lady Mayhew held her close for a moment longer, then pulled back, tugging out her handkerchief to wipe her eyes.

"Please, sit here, Lady Mayhew." Peter got to his feet, even though he would have much preferred to stay beside Miss Jennings. "Julia, thank goodness you are safe." Coming over to his sister, he embraced her and then stepped back. "What happened?"

Julia looked at him, her eyes wide with surprise. "Wait a moment before I answer, Denfield. Did you find Miss Jennings? Did you not return home?"

"No, I made my own way here." Miss Jennings spoke just before Peter had opportunity. "I have not told Lord Denfield as yet how I made my escape but I have every intention of doing so."

"I thought that could wait until some refreshment had been brought in," Peter added, quickly. "It should be coming in just a moment."

"I am afraid that we discovered nothing." Coming over to Miss Jennings, Julia reached down to embrace her. "Though I am so utterly delighted that you have returned to us. We have all been so very worried."

Miss Jennings' gaze went to Peter's and he nodded, though a faint flush crept up into his cheeks. Had their kiss not been interrupted, he would have told her about how he had come to realize that he loved her.

"Lord Symington has not returned as yet," Peter told Julia, seeing her frown gently. "I do hope he will appear soon."

"As do I, though perhaps with a better result than Lady Mayhew and I," came the response. "We did not even *see* the man with the bird cage."

"The man with the bird cage?" Miss Jennings repeated, leaving Peter to quickly explain what it was that had taken place. Miss Jennings' eyes grew round, though, after he had finished explaining, she frowned hard, her lips pursing.

"Mayhap it is that this gentleman – the one with the empty bird cage – was the one who owned the townhouse Lord Henley

143

took me to," she said, slowly. "It was not a house I recognised and when I made my escape from it, it was not in a part of London I knew."

The door opened and Peter looked up, ready to give a sharp word to whichever servant had come in without knocking, only for Lord Symington to make his way inside. He was beaming, perhaps having been informed by the butler that Miss Jennings was safe, for he went straight to the lady and taking her hand, bowed over it.

"How delighted I am to know that you are well," he said, as the servants came in behind him, setting down trays of food and another of tea and coffee. "I was informed the moment I stepped inside. Utterly marvelous, I must say."

"I thank you." Miss Jennings smiled and sat back. "I am very relieved to be here."

"You said you made your escape," Julia said, as she rose to start serving the tea. "What sort of house was it? Was it not a gentleman's house?"

Miss Jennings considered for a moment, then shook her head. "No, I would not say it was *not* a gentleman's house. It certainly was though it is situated in a part of London I do not know, as I have said."

"Perhaps a slightly lower situation, then?" Julia set the tea in front of Miss Jennings as she nodded.

"It was certainly a little smaller than the townhouse of my father," Miss Jennings replied, slowly. "Lord Henley locked me in one of the rooms but, the second time he stepped away – after providing me with something to eat and drink – he forgot to do so."

"Forgot?"

A slightly shy smile crossed Miss Jennings' face. "I may have made him very angry indeed and in his fury, he forgot to do as he intended. That was my hope and my intention, I confess, and it was successful. He *did* leave without locking the door – but then I became afraid that someone else was in the house."

Julia sat back down. "Because of what he had brought you. Did you perhaps think that there would be a servant?"

"Precisely – but there was not. In fact, the whole house was empty. I made my escape down the servants staircase and from there, outside... though I was very afraid that I would be discovered for at the very time I was about to hurry out of the house, Lord Henley returned."

Peter shook his head. "I am sorry that he did so much wrong to you."

"Might I ask how you found your way here?" Lady Mayhew asked, taking her niece's hand. "You did not know where you were, so... ?"

"I forced my way into a hackney where, much to my relief, I found a very kind lady and her husband. I did not tell them who I was or what had happened for fear of my reputation but the lady in particular was most generous and did not press me. Instead, she took me to where I requested to go, did not demand payment for the fare and I was able to return here."

"How very generous of them." Lady Mayhew closed her eyes. "I dare not even let myself imagine what would have been, had they not been so kind."

A slight shiver ran down Peter's spine. "Nor I."

"In which case, do not," Julia said, firmly. "So Henley knows you have made your escape."

"And he only has the fifty pounds you gave him," Lord Symington added, though Miss Jennings' eyebrows lifted at this. "There can be nothing else to concern us now, surely?"

Peter chewed on the edge of his lip for a moment and then, with a sigh, shook his head. "I do not think it will be as simple as simply putting this behind us. My brother is clearly quite determined to do whatever he can to force my hand, to do as *he* demands and simply because Miss Jennings is safe with us now does not mean that she will continue to be so."

"I would agree," Lady Mayhew replied, softly. "Even if you are wed, there is still enough reason for him to do the very same thing, should he be given opportunity."

"Which he would take, I am certain of it." Julia handed Peter a cup of coffee, having just placed a cup of tea on the table in front of Lady Mayhew. "We must do something, brother."

"But what?" Frustrated, Peter thought desperately of something he might enact which would stop Henley from behaving in such a way, from being such a threat to his own and Miss Jennings' happiness, but nothing came to mind. "I do not know what I am to do." Looking to Lord Symington, he lifted an eyebrow.

"Did you have any success in pursuing that gentleman? Is there a faint hope there that we might know who it is that is aiding him?"

After a few moments, Lord Symington nodded slowly, though his expression remained a little grim. "It is not entirely certain, though there is reason enough to think that the name I was given for this gentlemen is correct."

"The name you were given?" Julia asked, before Peter could do so. "What do you mean?"

Lord Symington quickly explained. "I followed the man with the bird cage though, after he glanced at me for the third time, I realised that he knew I was following him. I fell back, frustrated, understanding now that the man himself would be doing all he could to make certain I could not trail him to his destination – no doubt to give the fifty pounds to your brother, Denfield. To my relief, however, I saw an acquaintance I knew stopping to greet the man, though he was ignored, and therefore, I took my chance and asked that acquaintance who the gentleman was."

"And?"

In answer to Peter's question, Lord Symington smiled briefly. "My acquaintance stated that he believed it to be Lord Munslow – *Baron* Munslow, to be exact – though he said he could not be certain given the way he was ignored."

Another brief silence filled the room before Miss Jennings finally broke it. "If it was Baron Munslow, then might that be the reason for the slightly reduced townhouse? Could it be *his* townhouse I stayed in?"

"It could very well be." Lady Mayhew took her niece's hand. "You have done very well, Anne, but I insist that you rest now. You have endured a great deal and you must be exhausted."

Miss Jennings smiled quickly and confirmed that yes, she was fatigued, but it was not without a slight worry flickering in her eyes. Peter pressed his lips together, seeing the way Julia fixed a fervent gaze upon him, realizing that he was expected to either do or say something.

"Might I suggest that everyone resides here overnight?" he asked, looking back at Julia and then over to Lady Mayhew and Miss Jennings. "I feel it would be safest for everyone to do so – and if you stay here with Miss Jennings, Lady Mayhew, and my sister and Lord Symington do also, then the servants will have nothing to gossip about... though I fully intend to make certain that they do not gossip regardless. That is, if they want to keep their positions."

Miss Jennings nodded so quickly and with such fervency, it was clear that the thought brought her a great deal of relief. "Yes, I should like that very much, Lord Denfield. It is not to say that I would not feel safe back at home but – "

"But given that my brother is unpredictable and has already done something dreadful, you fear that he might attempt to do something even more wicked," Peter finished for her, seeing the slight glistening in her eyes and recognizing the worry there. "I shall have rooms made up at once. Perhaps by tomorrow morning, we will have come up with a plan to stop my brother from pursuing this dark path." Seeing the doubt in Lord Symington's eyes and the way his sister bit her lip, Peter spread out both hands. "We can only hope."

Chapter Twenty-Three

Anne sighed and swung her legs over the side of the bed. It had been a long afternoon and she had been glad to go and rest but now that the dinner gong would soon be called, she had a desire to rise and be in company again. The few hours she had spent under Lord Henley's power had been more than enough and the joy and relief that came with being back in Lord Denfield's arms and in the company of her aunt was almost overwhelming.

"You are awake."

Looking up, Anne smiled as the door was pushed all the way open and her aunt came inside. "Yes, Aunt. I had a restful sleep and feel a good deal more refreshed."

"I am glad." Lady Mayhew came closer and took one of her hands in hers. "Lord Denfield has been unable to sit at pace since you went to rest. I am sure he will be delighted to see you looking so much better." Reaching out, she patted Anne's cheek gently. "You did look so very pale."

Anne acknowledged this with a nod and a smile. "I am sure he shall be." She did not say a word to her aunt about the kiss Lord Denfield and she had shared, nor tell her of the tenderness and affection he had spoken of to her just before her aunt and Lady Symington had arrived. All the same, the joy of that wrapped around Anne's heart and her smile grew all the more. "I should like to go down to him, if we might?"

"Of course. Just let me call the maid to come first." Making her way across the room, Lady Mayhew rang the bell and then gestured for Anne to sit down at the dressing table. "You will need to have your hair fixed and perhaps a new gown, since you have not changed since you returned."

Anne flushed. "I do not have another gown."

"Ah, but I had some things brought," came the quick reply. "While you were resting, I had a few personal items retrieved and two of your best gowns."

"Thank you, Aunt." Turning to look at her reflection, Anne took in the shadows under her eyes and quickly pinched her cheeks to bring a little more color to her face. "I should like to look my best for Lord Denfield."

"But he does not care what you look like, given that you are already well settled within his heart," her aunt replied, gently. "Do not protest, my dear, or pretend that you do not care for him as much as he cares for you! It is only of my greatest joys to see you so contented." Her lips puckered, her happiness fading. "If only Lord Denfield could think of a way to stop his dreadful brother from doing anything akin to this again!"

Anne nodded, just as the maid knocked and then came in. "I am sure that he will be doing everything possible, Aunt. And I have every faith that, in time, he will come up with a solution."

***

"I am glad to see you looking so much better." Lord Denfield sat down next to Anne, his eyes settling on hers, a smile on his lips. "You appear refreshed at least, though I am sure that there is still a great deal of concern over what Henley might try next."

Anne knew how much he wanted her to be truthful and, with a small shrug, spoke from the heart. "I am a little concerned but remaining here with you, staying under your roof and with your protection, I know that I am quite safe and secure. That brings me a good deal of relief."

"I am glad to hear it." Lord Denfield smiled and took her hand, which she gave willingly. "Perhaps we should marry sooner, Miss Jennings... Anne. Perhaps we should marry tomorrow!"

She blinked. "Tomorrow?"

"In this house, with your family and mine as witnesses," he said, though he frowned as he spoke. "It would not be my desire, however, for we have each made plans for our day in church but I do wonder if it would change my brother's attitude in any way."

Anne considered this, not wanting to refuse immediately but at the same time, doing her best to understand the desire behind it. "You yourself said, however, that your brother would not be constrained simply because we are wed."

"That is true." Lord Denfield ran one hand over his chin. "It is more, perhaps, because you would be protected and a little *more* secure, I suppose." His thumb ran over the back of her hand. "You would not have to return home, for example. You would be able to reside here, to stay with me."

149

The thought was a pleasing one, though the blush it brought to Anne's cheeks and the heat which seared through her forced her to look away from him for just a moment. "You are very considerate, Lord Denfield, and I should be glad of any further protection, certainly. Though," she continued, able to look into his eyes again, "I should not like to be forced into a course of action simply because of your brother's threat. To my mind, that would not be a wise response. I say this also because we have both worked hard to prepare the wedding day, have we not? It is not too far from us now."

Lord Denfield let out a slow breath and then nodded. "You are quite right, though I should like you to know that my desire to marry you has only grown. The day could not come any more quickly!" His fingers pressed through hers and Anne smiled back at him, her heart filled with a happiness that she did not think she could express, not even should she be given all the words in all the world.

"I care for you, Denfield." It was not what she had meant to say, not truly what she wanted to say, but the words came from her heart regardless. She blinked, looking back into his face and seeing him smile big and bright, his eyes shining.

"I did not think that we would ever be in such a state of happiness," he told her, softly so that the others in the room would not hear him. "When I stepped into that space between my brother and yourself, when I told those gossiping ladies that we were engaged, I never once imagined that we would be as contented as we are now – that I would be *eager* for the day of our marriage! I did not think that our hearts would be filled with an affection for each other and I confess myself to be overwhelmingly grateful for it."

"As am I," Anne sighed, contentedly. "Even there has been a great deal of trial and a depth of fear, I confess that it has made my heart grow all the more in affection for you, Lord Denfield. When I was alone in that room, when I was left without escape, the only person I could think of, my only desire, was for you and to be in your arms again." She thought that there would be a flush of embarrassment rising up within her given the bluntness with which she spoke and the honesty of her words but instead, all she felt was joy. Joy at being able to share with him what she truly felt and gladness in knowing that he felt the very same way.

"I will say that – "

A knock at the door interrupted Lord Denfield from whatever it was he had been about to say and as he called for the servant to enter, his hand left Anne's.

"This arrived for you, my lord." The butler handed the letter to Lord Denfield. "It was to be given to you at once."

Lord Denfield frowned but took it, breaking the seal and then unfolding the letter. Sitting down, he read it and then looked up sharply at the waiting butler. "Who brought this?"

"A man I did not recognise," the butler said, quietly. "He ran from the house once it was delivered."

"Who is it from?" Anne asked, seeing the worry etching itself across his expression.

"It is Henley?" Lady Symington rose to her feet and came across the room towards Lord Denfield, though Anne chose to remain where she sat, not wanting to rise to her feet and join brother and sister. "What does he say?"

Lord Denfield said nothing for some minutes, then took in a deep breath and looked down at Anne. "He is angry that you made your escape."

"I am sure that he is," Lady Symington murmured, looking down to Anne and then back to Lord Denfield. "What else does he say?"

Lord Denfield shook his head. "He demands a great deal of money from me."

"For what purpose?" Anne asked, fright catching in her chest. "Why should he ask for money?"

Lady Symington closed her eyes. "He must be in deep difficulty financially – more than we knew."

"He states that it must be paid otherwise my bride to be will be prevented from reaching the church on the day of our marriage." Lord Denfield let out a long, slow breath, though Anne saw how one hand curled up into a tight fist. Clearly the man was angry – angry with his brother, angry with his demands – but he was doing his utmost to keep his temper.

"Then we do as you suggested," she said, quickly, though Lord Denfield quickly shook his head.

"No, my dear Anne," he said, coming to sit back down beside

151

her, reaching to take her hand again. "No, we cannot. Even if we were to marry tomorrow or the day after that, I am sure that the threat my brother presents will never cease. Not unless I do something more. Not unless I make a stand and find a way to make sure that he can never come to near to us again."

Anne looked into his eyes, her hand tightening on his. "What do you mean to do?"

"I mean to give him a choice," Lord Denfield said, firmly, as everyone in the room turned their attention to him, ready to take in what it was he said. "Either I will call him out – and he will accept and be in danger of his life – or he will make his way to the continent and inspect his holdings there, making them profitable enough for him."

Anne's eyes flared, fright burning through her. "You would call out your own brother? You would think to injure him? To be in danger of killing him?"

Lord Denfield looked back at her steadily, his gaze fixed but his jaw tight. "I swear, should he accept, I will do my utmost to make sure that I only injure him. But he has to understand that this cannot continue. I will *not* simply accept his threats and presume to do as he asks. I have to draw a line, Anne. I *have* to make him understand that you will be the one I defend, you will be the one I will protect. I will not be swayed, I will not be coerced, I will not be pushed one way or the other by my brother's hands. No, I will stand up for what is right, for what I know I must protect and I will do it willingly."

"I will be your second." Lord Symington rose to his feet and walked across the room to stand beside his wife, one arm going around her waist as she set fearful eyes to him. "I quite agree with you, Denfield. Tell him also that Lord Munslow should be his second – *show* him that you know of his ploys! Force must be used, be it either verbal or physical. It cannot be any other way."

Anna swallowed hard, wishing that there could be another way but realizing that what Lord Denfield had decided was right. If force was to be the only way that Lord Henley would change, would stop him from this pursuit of both his brother's and her wealth, then so be it.

"I do not want to be so close to you, so near to being your wife, only to lose you," she whispered, her voice shaking with emotion as she looked into his eyes. "I am afraid of what will happen if you do this."

Silence rang around the room for a few moments, only for Lady Symington to smile and, coming closer to Anne, to settle one hand on her shoulder.

"Do not fear," she said, quietly. "My brother Henley is a gentleman who lacks bravery. He has not shown courage in any way thus far. He has had his friend do his part in collecting the first lot of money from my brother. He has hidden you away, a young lady without support, and has done nothing other than write a few letters to Denfield. I feel quite confident that, should this be written to Lord Henley, he will show no courage and will turn away from this entirely."

Anne felt the comfort from Lady Symington and saw the reassurance in Lord Denfield's eyes and slowly, her worry faded just a little. "Very well," she said, softly. "Do what you must, Lord Denfield. But I pray that you come back to me safe and well for I could not bear to be parted from you again."

Chapter Twenty-Four

Peter finished writing his letter and, with a scowl, made to seal it. Melting the wax, he considered what his brother had written, the demands he had made and found his heart sinking with despair. Was this truly who Henley had become? A man who was so inclined towards selfishness that he would do whatever he could to gain what he wanted? That was not the brother that Peter knew and it was certainly not the brother that he *wanted*.

"Am I being too harsh?"

Lord Symington pushed open the door to Peter's study just as Peter spoke aloud. Hearing it, he quickly shook his head.

"No, you are not being too harsh. This has to be done."

"I am giving him a choice between losing his life or saving it by leaving England and going to the continent. Both of them push him away from me."

"Which he has brought upon himself," Lord Symington reminded him, walking across the room to pour himself a brandy and then another measure for Peter. "You have always been a very caring, considerate, respectful and kindhearted gentleman, especially when it comes to family. You have spent the last few years pursuing your brother, coming to his aid and sorting his difficulties for him, both in the hope of making him consider his actions *and* in protecting your family name." Handing Peter the glass, he lifted his shoulders and shrugged. "That has changed. It is difficult for you, yes, but it must be done."

Peter nodded and pushed his ring into the wax, sealing the letter. His shoulders dropped, his heart heavy. "At one time, I would have done anything for Henley. I would have taken any action to try and protect him and, as you have said, to protect my family name. Now, however, I realise, that I must let my brother do as he wishes. It must be his choice." Lifting his head, he looked straight back into Lord Symington's face. "And I have someone I care about a good deal more."

Lord Symington nodded. "You love her."

"I do. I just have not told her as yet." Picking up the letter, he walked across the room to ring the bell. "I must hope that Henley will take the latter option, though I am not certain."

"Let me take it." Lord Symington stepped forward and reached out one hand to take the letter. "I will take the letter to Henley, make certain he reads it and find out what it is he will do. Thereafter, I will make certain of it, even if I have to follow him down to the docks!"

Peter hesitated. "That is a lot for you to do. I should not like to put you in danger."

"I do not fear your brother and indeed, I should be very pleased – glad, even – to do this for you. It will protect you, Miss Jennings *and* Julia. Please. Let me do this."

Seeing the fervor in Lord Symington's eyes, Peter thanked him and then handed the letter to him. Without a word and only a brief nod instead, Lord Symington stepped out of the room, leaving Peter alone.

Letting out a sigh, Peter closed his eyes and lowered his head. There was nothing else to be done, nothing else he could even think to do to sort out the situation. The letter was written, the demands were made.

All he could do now was wait.

**

Peter woke up violently as a sound startled him awake. His stiff neck made him cry out just as the door opened and the face of Miss Jennings appeared in the doorway.

"Forgive me," she began to say, only for Peter to stand up from his chair and beckon her in, ignoring the way his body cried out in pain.

"Please, come in." Rubbing the back of his neck, he could not help but let out a low groan. "I must have fallen asleep in my chair."

Miss Jennings hid a smile, though her expression remained one of sympathy. "You could not sleep?"

He shook his head. "I was waiting for Symington to return from delivering my note to Henley," he said, reaching out to take her hand. "He must not have returned as yet."

"No, he is here already," Miss Jennings told him, coming to stand a little closer to him – and Peter closed his eyes, inhaling the scent she brought to him. It was of sweetness, of honey or blossom

155

– he did not know which. Either way, he found himself desperate to be closer to her and, wrapping one arm around her waist, tugged her nearer to him. Miss Jennings giggled, a blush coming into her cheeks though she smiled up at him rather than turning her head away. "You did not hear what I said, I think."

Peter frowned. "No, I do not think I did. You are much too distracting, Anne." When he bent his head to kiss her, she was already waiting for him, a soft sigh escaping her as his lips touched hers. He had not heard at all what she had said, had found himself caught up with the desire to be close to her, to take all of her into himself and hold her tight. Heat shot up through his core and he pulled himself back reluctantly. This was not the moment for such things – especially when he had more to say to her, more to confess about the state of his heart.

"Should you... " Miss Jennings let out a slow sigh of contentment, making Peter smile as her eyes fluttered closed. "Should you like me to repeat what I said?"

"I suppose you should," he grinned, wishing silently that they might keep themselves together just here, just for a little longer. "I did not hear it the first time."

Miss Jenings smiled at him. "I said that Lord Symington has already returned. He offered to come to see if he could find you here, given that the butler assured us you were not in your rooms. However, given that he is rather fatigued, I thought to come and look in your study myself."

A jolt ran up Peter's spine. "I am very glad that you did," he said, though he did begin to move back from her. "But Symington has returned, you say?"

"Yes, though not more than fifteen minutes ago."

Peter squeezed her hand. "Come, I should go to see him at once. He took the note to Henley, you see. He must have received an answer from him."

Miss Jennings' smile froze to her face, her eyes rounding. "Lord Symington took the note directly?"

"Yes, he did." Coming close to her again, Peter smiled gently. "Have no fear, he will not have come back without an answer from Henley." Battling down his own anxiety, his own nervousness, he tugged her carefully towards the door. "Come now. Let us see what it is that Symington has to tell us."

They walked together in silence – albeit, comfortable silence – until they reached the dining room. Stepping inside, Peter walked immediately to the table, his eyes fixed to Lord Symington's rather pale, tired face. "Symington? You look exhausted. I pray you were successful, however?"

Lord Symington took a quick sip of his coffee and then nodded. "I was."

Peter led Miss Jennings to a chair and then sat down beside her, though he barely took his gaze from Lord Symington. "What did you discover?"

"That your brother is an arrogant fool," Lord Symington replied, sharply, his brows furrowing as he looked away from Peter for a moment. "Forgive me for saying it so bluntly but I must be honest."

"I quite understand."

Lord Symington's gaze returned to him. "I told you I would not return without an answer and he has given it."

"Oh?"

Lord Symington lifted his chin. "I accompanied him in the early hours of the morning down to the docks. I watched him purchase his ticket and I remained at the port until the ship taking him had departed."

Peter stared at his friend, his mouth a little ajar. His whole body had grown cold, his heart seeming to stop in his chest for a moment as he stared at Lord Symington, hardly daring to believe it.

"He was so incredibly arrogant when I first arrived," Lord Symington continued, evidently seeing Peter's shock and realizing that he ought to explain. "I had to force my way inside – something I am not proud of but given that my stature is a little greater than your brother's, I did not find it particularly difficult."

"His butler did not stop you?"

"He had no butler, only a footman and one maid." Lord Symington's eyebrows lifted. "It appears that Lord Henley has been a little more out of coin than he expressed to us."

Peter closed his eyes. "Goodness."

"As I said, he mocked me *and* you and did not believe the contents of the letter. When I made myself very plain, telling him that I expected to return to this house with news of who his second was, he slowly began to realize the gravity of the situation. When I

157

mentioned Lord Munslow, he then realized that we knew all who had been involved with him and that there was no means of escape. Thereafter, he slowly began to sink into his chair and looked so utterly overcome, I believe the shock of your letter finally began to take hold."

"And therefore, he decided to go to the continent?" Lady Symington asked, as her husband nodded. "Just like that?"

Lord Symington's lip curled upwards just a little. "I did make it plain that I would forcibly drag him to the grounds for pistols at dawn if he did not make a choice and that seemed to put an end to it. He packed a few thing – under my supervision, of course, for I did not want him to make his escape – and then we departed for the docks. It is done, Denfield. Your brother is gone to the continent and whenever he should have the funds to return, I think he will be a very changed man. He sees now that you are no longer the brother he once knew – not that I think that to be a bad thing but rather a heartily good change – and therefore will have a good deal to consider during his time away."

Peter swallowed hard and, reaching across the table, shook Lord Symington's hand firmly. "Thank you, Symington. You cannot know what this means to me." His gaze then went to Miss Jennings, seeing her damp eyes and, before he could stop himself, Peter was out of his chair and had pulled her up tight into his arms. She let out a slightly broken sob and though he hated the sound of it, though he was upset at the cause of it, he could not help but rejoice that the matter was at an end.

"It is over," he said hoarsely, as Lady Mayhew pulled out her handkerchief to dab at her eyes. "You are safe. *We* are safe." Pulling back, he looked into Miss Jennings' eyes. "And we will be married just as we planned. What say you to that?"

Miss Jennings smiled, her hand settling just at his heart as she blinked away the last of her tears. "I can think of nothing better."

Epilogue

"Anne?"

Anne let out a squeal of surprise as Lord Denfield's voice filled the room. "Denfield! We are not meant to see each other before our vows!" A sudden worry filled her and she turned to face him a little more. "Is there something wrong?"

"Nothing." Lord Denfield's smile was tender as he swept her up into his arms. "It is only that I had something I wanted to tell you – two things, in fact – before we made our way to the church."

"Oh." Anne let out a slow breath, her shoulders dropping, her frame softening as he held her in his arms. "What is it that you wanted to say?"

Lord Denfield dropped his head and kissed her lightly, though it was only for a moment and certainly not long enough for her to lose herself in it. "I firstly wanted to tell you that I love you, Anne."

She blinked. "You love me?"

"I do. With all of my heart." Sighing contentedly, his arms tightened around her a little more. "I love you so very much, I cannot even think of containing those words within my heart! I have wanted to tell you for some time but there has never seemed to be an opportunity! So I determined to tell you of my heart before we wed, even if it was only an hour before we made our way to the church!"

Anne's heart exploded with joy. "I love *you*, Denfield."

His eyes flared. "You love me in return?"

"Of course I do. How could I not?" she told him, her heart still overwhelmed with all that he had offered her, all that he had *given* her. "You are the most wonderful of gentlemen, the most kind, considerate, courageous and upright gentleman and my heart is truly yours."

He kissed her then, kissed her softly and sweetly and Anne felt herself melt into his arms, her breathing quickening as their kiss of shared love made a true impact upon her heart.

"I should take my leave." Lord Denfield breathed, forcing a tiny inch of space between them, clearly as reluctant as she was to step away.

"I suppose you must, if we are to wed," she answered, a quiet laugh in her voice. "Though, Denfield, was it not that you had two things you wished to share with me?"

Lord Denfield nodded, pulling himself back all the more and looking down into her eyes. "There is. Give me a moment."

Anne watched in confusion as he stepped away from her, walking back towards the door. Opening it, he went through it and stayed away from her for some moments, though his hand remained on the door handle. Anne was about to step closer, about to find out what it was that he was doing when the door opened and he came back towards her.

"I wanted to do something for you," he told her, taking her hand in his again. "I wanted to make sure that your happiness was complete on our wedding day."

Looking into his face, Anne fought to understand what he meant. "I am already happy."

"But I am sure you will be all the more so," he said, turning and gesturing to the door – just as, to Anne's utter astonishment, her mother walked through the door.

She stopped, her hands going to her mouth, her eyes flooded with tears as Anne stared at her, hardly able to believe that she was present.

"Your father knows nothing of this," Lord Denfield said softly. "There is nothing to be afraid of."

"Mama." Anne's voice was a choked sob as she released his hand and slowly began to make her way towards her mother, her hands outstretched as Lady Ellon reached out to embrace her. To be held tightly in her mother's arms was almost too wonderful to believe, almost too astonishing to take in and Anne immediately began to weep.

"I am here, my darling Anne," her mother whispered, her own voice hoarse with emotion. "I am so sorry I have been away for so long."

"No, there are to be no apologies, Mama," Anne replied immediately, pulling back so she could look into her mother's face. "I understand."

Her mother's eyes filled with tears. "You do?"

"Of course I do," Anne replied, quickly, her own vision a little blurred with her own happy tears. "I would not be where I am

160

today without my aunt's help. I understand why you have had to stay away."

"But she is here now." Lord Denfield came over to them both and, putting a hand around Anne's waist, smiled into her eyes. "And she will be here with us on our wedding day... and longer, if you both wish it."

Anne did not understand for a moment, a slight frown on her face. "What do you mean?"

"I would be very glad indeed to have you reside with us, Lady Ellon," Lord Denfield said, before turning back to Anne. "I understand the reason behind the separation and I will support it. If your mother wishes to reside with us at the Denfield estate, there is *more* than enough space for her to reside here for as long as she wishes."

Anne could not speak for a moment, such was her joy. "You would do this?"

"Of course I would, because I love you," came the reply. "And should Lord Ellon ever attempt to come and force your return, Lady Ellon," he continued, turning back to Anne's mother, "then you can be assured that I would do everything to stand in the way of that, and to make sure that you are safe and protected."

The love Anne held in her heart for Lord Denfield grew to such proportions, she could barely even think. Her heart swelled and she leaned into him, her head on his shoulder as, blinking away yet more joyous tears, she looked to her mother. "Will you, Mama?" she asked, hope over hope abounding as she saw her mother smile.

"I should be delighted to accept that offer," came the reply, as Anne's smile split her face. "Thank you, Lord Denfield."

"Yes, thank you, Denfield," Anne whispered, looking up into his face and wondering to herself just how she could love this gentleman any more than she did already. "You have brought everything to me and I am overwhelmed by it."

"As I am overwhelmed by you," he whispered, gently. "I love you, Anne."

"And I love you."

***

The clergyman opened the book of Common Prayer, his expression one of solemnity which added to the weightiness of the moment. Anne dared a glance at Lord Denfield but he was looking away from her, his gaze trained upon the clergyman and with a serious expression on his face, clearly sensing the solemnity of their situation just as she did. His eyes turned to hers for just a moment however, and the happiness which grew up within her crept to such great heights, it pushed the corners of her mouth up regardless. She had never imagined that she would find herself wed this Season, had never thought that the gentleman who had saved her from a difficult situation would soon become someone she loved with all of her heart!

The clergyman cleared his throat, looked first to Lord Denfield, then to Anne. This was a little unusual, Anne suspected, given that her father was not present – but oh, the joy of having her mother with them! The clergyman would not have to ask who would give her to join in marriage with Lord Denfield, given that she was of age, and that brought such a fresh sense of joy that Anne's face split with a smile, just as the clergyman began.

"Dearly beloved, we are gathered together here in the sight of God, and in the face of this congregation to join together this Man and this Woman in holy Matrimony, which is an honorable estate, instituted of God in the time of man's innocence, signifying unto us the mystical union that is between Christ and his Church. It is not to be taken on unadvisedly, lightly, or wantonly, to satisfy men's carnal lusts and but reverently, discreetly, advisedly, soberly, and in the fear of God; duly considering the causes for which Matrimony was ordained."

The clergyman continued on and Anne closed her eyes, taking in every single word that was said. It was as if she wanted to cling to each moment for a little longer, to hold onto it so that she might fully take it in. This was the moment she would be bound to Lord Denfield forever, where she would become his wife – and where her father, unwittingly, of course, would no longer be able to demand that she do as *he* demanded. She was to be bound to Lord Denfield, yes, but that in itself brought such a freedom, it was quite overwhelming.

"First," the clergyman intoned, "marriage was ordained for the procreation of children, to be brought up in the fear and nurture of the Lord, and to the praise of his holy Name. Secondly, it was ordained for a remedy against sin and thirdly, it was ordained for the mutual society, help, and comfort that the one ought to have of the other, both in prosperity and adversity. God Almighty, into which holy estate these two persons present come now to be joined. Therefore if any man can show any just cause, why they may not lawfully be joined together, let him now speak, or else hereafter forever hold his peace."

Anne glanced to her right and to her left, knowing full well that there was no-one there to protest. All the same, a little bird seemed to flutter in her heart, perhaps fearful that her father had somehow found out and would throw himself into the church and demand an end to this union – though that soon faded away as silence met the clergyman's words. Lord Denfield shifted on his feet, his eyes darting to hers for a moment and, as she returned his gaze, he finally offered her a small smile. Her heart sang.

The clergyman looked to them both again, clearly satisfied that there was no protestations and that the marriage ceremony could continue. "I require and charge you both, as you will answer at the dreadful day of judgement when the secrets of all hearts shall be disclosed, that if either of you know any impediment why you may not be lawfully joined together in Matrimony, you now confess it. For be you well assured, that so many as are coupled together otherwise than God's Word doth allow are not joined together by God; neither is their Matrimony lawful."

Anne looked steadily back at the clergyman, nothing in her heart or mind that might bring any guilt to her conscience. Lord Denfield too remained silent and, with a nod, the clergyman looked back to the book of Common Prayer again.

"Lord Denfield, will you have this woman to thy wedded wife, to live together after God's ordinance in the holy estate of Matrimony? Will you love her, comfort her, honour, and keep her in sickness and in health; and, forsaking all other, keep yourself only to her, so long as you both shall live?"

Lord Denfield looked to Anne, that tender smile spreading right across his face now. "I will."

The clergyman did not smile, however, keeping his expression serious as he fulfilled his duties. "Miss Anne Jennings, will you have this man to thy wedded husband, to live together after God's ordinance in the holy estate of Matrimony? Will you obey him, and serve him, love, honour, and keep him in sickness and in health; and, forsaking all others, keep yourself only to him, so long as you both shall live?

Taking in a deep breath, Anne lifted her chin just a little. "I will."

"I thank you." The clergyman reached out and, in lieu of there being a father or brother to offer her hand to Lord Denfield's, took Anne's hand and, carefully and quickly, set it upon Lord Denfield's. Anne's heart leapt with joy as Lord Denfield smiled down at her, the heat from his hand rushing up into her arm and onwards into her heart.

"Lord Denfield," the clergyman gestured to him. "In sight of this congregation and in the eyes of God, speak your vows to Miss Anne Jennings."

Lord Denfield turned so he might look at her fully. The tenderness in his expression, the softness about his eyes and the gentle smile on his lips had her desiring to throw her arms about him and hold him close though she fought the urge fiercely. Now was not the moment for such things.

"Miss Anne Jennings, I take you as my wedded wife, to have and to hold from this day forward, for better for worse, for richer for poorer, in sickness and in health, to love and to cherish, till death us do part, according to God's holy ordinance."

"And you now, Miss Anne Jennings, make your vows to Lord Denfield."

The words could not spin from her mouth any more quickly. "Peter, Earl of Denfield, I take you to be my wedded husband, to have and to hold from this day forward, for better for worse, for richer for poorer, in sickness and in health, to love, cherish, and to obey, till death us do part, according to God's holy ordinance."

Lord Denfield smiled back at her and Anne's hand tightened on his, her joy so near to completion.

"We come the giving and receiving of the ring." The clergyman gestured to Lord Denfield and, without a momentary hesitation, he took the ring from his pocket and pushed it onto the third finger of her left hand.

"Miss Anne Jennings," he murmured, quietly, "with this ring I thee wed. With my body I thee worship, and with all my worldly goods I thee endow."

Anne looked down to their joined hands, taking in the gold ring which now sat on her finger. It declared that she was bound to Lord Denfield and he to her. It was a reminder of the promises they had made to each other, both before the congregation and before God. How much she would cherish it! How much it represented!

Lifting his hand by way of a blessing, the clergyman led them all in a final prayer. "Eternal God, Creator and Preserver of all mankind, Giver of all spiritual grace, the Author of everlasting life: Send thy blessing upon these thy servants, this man and this woman, whom we bless in thy Name; that, as Isaac and Rebecca lived faithfully together, so these persons may surely perform and keep the vow and covenant between them made, whereof this Ring given and received is a token and pledge, and may ever remain in perfect love and peace together, and live according to thy laws; through Jesus Christ our Lord. Amen."

"Amen," she whispered, just as the clergyman put his hand on top of hers, as it rested on Lord Denfield's. The final moment had come.

"Those whom God hath joined together let no man put asunder," the clergyman finished, raising his hand to gesture to those sitting in the congregation. "In as much as Lord Denfield and Miss Anne Jennings have consented together in holy wedlock and have witnessed the same before God and this company, and thereto have given and pledged their troth either to other and have declared the same by giving and receiving of a Ring, and by joining of hands; I pronounce that they be Man and Wife together. In the Name of the Father, and of the Son, and of the Holy Ghost. Amen."

Anne wanted to let out a cry of delight and happiness but there was nothing but silence to greet her. She closed her eyes and let out a slow breath, overcome with the sheer love and joy which not only built up within her but also seemed to spread out from within her, right to the very tips of her fingers. She looked up at Lord Denfield, seeing how his eyes shone with gladness and felt her own heart leap.

"Your marriage lines," the clergyman murmured, gesturing for them to follow him through to a quieter room to the back of the church. "And then you will be able to greet your friends and family."

Anne permitted Lord Denfield to lead her away, casting a quick glance over her shoulder to where her mother was sitting, Lady Mayhew on one side and Lady Symington on the other. She was dabbing lightly at her eyes though her smile was sparkling, echoing the happiness in Anne's own heart. The kindness of Lord Denfield in even thinking to arrange her mother's presence here was something she could still not fully take in, wondering at the sweetness, the tenderness of his heart towards her.

"Just in here, Lady Denfield."

It was the first time she had ever been referred to by her new title and it took Anne a moment to realise that the clergyman was speaking to her. With a gentle laugh, she looked up at Lord Denfield. "I quite forgot that I am to be Lady Denfield now."

"You are," he replied, a gentle gleam in his eye as he pulled her tight against him for a moment, though she was quickly released given the clergyman's presence. Struggling to pull herself away from her new husband, Anne sat down at the chair offered to her and, picking up the quill, signed her name where the clergyman indicated. Soon, it was completed and once Lord Denfield had done the same, the clergyman smiled, clearly delighted that all had gone well.

"My heartiest congratulations to you both," he said, gesturing to the door. "And may God's blessing be upon your marriage."

Anne curtsied, wishing to show respect and gratitude. "I thank you. We are truly grateful for your service to us."

Lord Denfield murmured the same and, thereafter, led her to the door so they might walk through the church and then out to greet their waiting friends and family. The door shut behind them and, seeing the church empty, Anne could not help but turn to him, her hand going to his arm, the other to rest gently above his heart. "Oh, Denfield. I wanted to pause for a moment so it is just you and I... so that I might tell you again how much I have come to love you."

Lord Denfield's eyes softened immediately, his hand lifting to cup her cheek, her skin burning as his fingers brushed her skin. "And I cannot deny my heart. My heart tells me that I am in love with you also, Anne. I love you so very much." Lowering his head,

Lord Denfield caught her lips with his for only a brief moment, though it was long enough to have her sighing with contentment and longing for more – more of him, more of this moment, more of this happiness.

"Denfield," she whispered, keeping her face close, her eyes gazing into his. "My heart is yours."

"Then we are one." Smiling, he traced the curve of her jaw with gentle fingers. "No matter what takes place, no matter what the future shall bring us, I will always love you with every part of my heart, my soul, my very being. I love you, Anne, and I promise that I always shall."

THE END

Made in the USA
Monee, IL
26 April 2024